The door to her room opened.

Nick.

His steps were slow, measured, as he boldly approached her. He reached the foot of her bed and shook the robe he wore from his shoulders, let it puddle at his feet, then crawled onto the bed like a panther stalking its prey.

Nick stared deep into her eyes. Not a word had been spoken.

Sam watched as though mesmerized as he pulled down the sheet and exposed every inch of her body. He took a finger and slid it lazily from the heel of her foot to the insides of her thighs.

Sam lay back against the fluffy pillows. He kissed a sensitive spot behind her knee before trailing kisses up the insides of her thighs. Sam felt short of breath and tried to get away lest she die from pleasure. But Nick wasn't having it.

He was just getting started.

* * *

The Last Little Secret by Zuri Day is part of the Sin City Secrets series.

Dear Reader,

As a writer, I strive to always deliver amazing, sensual, page-turning love stories. Admittedly, though, some characters seem to come through better than others. Okay, if you promise to keep it between us, I'll be even more honest by letting you in on a secret. I have favorites. I know! It's like admitting favoring one child more than another. It's not supposed to happen. But it can't be helped.

I always knew Nick would be a lot of fun to write and couldn't wait to share his story. He didn't disappoint, especially with a pistol of a woman like Sam coming back into his life and changing his plans. Making him rearrange his priorities and take another look at what he thought was most important in life. He isn't alone in this moment of rediscovery. Sam is in for a surprise or two, as well.

Ending the Sin City Secrets series feels a bit bittersweet. I wasn't sure any family could outdo the Drakes of California, but the Breedlove Nevadans won me over. Writing their stories allowed me to share some of what I discovered in the two years I lived near Las Vegas, to showcase the desert's beauty and venture into what happens beyond downtown Fremont or The Strip. I hope you will enjoy Nick's story as much as you did those of Christian, Adam and Noah. If so, please leave a review and drop me a line at zuriday.com. If you visit Sin City, send a pic!

Until next time, much love and as always...

Have a zuri day!

Zuri

ZURI DAY

—

THE LAST LITTLE SECRET

HARLEQUIN
DESIRE

DESIRE™

ISBN-13: 978-1-335-23291-5

The Last Little Secret

Copyright © 2021 by Zuri Day

Recycling programs
for this product may
not exist in your area.

This edition published by arrangement with Harlequin Books S.A.

For questions and comments about the quality of this book,
please contact us at CustomerService@Harlequin.com.

Harlequin Enterprises ULC
22 Adelaide St. West, 40th Floor
Toronto, Ontario M5H 4E3, Canada
www.Harlequin.com

Printed in U.S.A.

Zuri Day is the award-winning, nationally bestselling author of a slew of novels translated into almost a dozen languages. When not writing, which is almost never, or traveling internationally, these days not so much, she can be found in the weeds, literally, engaged in her latest passion—gardening. Living in Southern California, this happens year-round. From there it's farm to table (okay, patio to table—it's an urban garden) via her creative culinary take on a variety of vegan dishes. She loves live performances (including her own), binges on popular YouTube shows and is diligently at work to make her Ragdoll cat, Namaste, the IG star he deserves to be. Say meow to him, stay in touch with her and check out her exhaustive stash of OMG reads at zuriday.com.

Books by Zuri Day

Harlequin Desire

Sin City Secrets

Sin City Vows
Ready for the Rancher
Sin City Seduction
The Last Little Secret

Visit her Author Profile page at Harlequin.com, or zuriday.com, for more titles.

You can also find Zuri Day on Facebook, along with other Harlequin Desire authors, at Facebook.com/harlequindesireauthors!

For we hopeful romantics
who know love always wins

No matter the challenges
when the journey begins

Love exposes our secrets,
a new world to unfold.

While nourishing our bodies
and filling our souls.

One

"Mr. Breedlove, your two o'clock is here."

"Thanks. Send her in."

"Will do."

"Hold my calls, Anita. I don't want to be interrupted."

"Got it, boss."

Nick shut off the intercom and second-guessed his decision for the fifth or sixth time. For a decisive man like Nick Breedlove, that didn't happen often. Hands down, Samantha Price was one of the best interior designers in the business, the only one he'd put complete confidence in to get him and the company out of an impossible jam. That she had become available was nothing short of a miracle. Hiring her was no doubt a sound business decision but personally, was it wise? He heard a soft knock and braced himself. If seeing her again caused the same reaction as last time, he might lose control of the meeting before it began. It had been more than four years but the memories from that night flooded his mind as though they'd happened just yesterday. The door opened. There she was. In the flesh. More beautiful than he remembered.

He stood, with hand outstretched. "Hello, Sam. It's been a long time."

"Hey, Nick," Sam replied, her smile tight yet polite as she clasped his hand ever so briefly while maintaining a good distance between them.

Was she remembering, too? Was the attraction that threatened to tighten his groin and quicken his breathing a mutual situation?

"I appreciate you coming on such short notice," he managed, a 007 coolness hiding a set of hormones suddenly raging as if he were fifteen instead of the twenty-seven he'd turned just a few short months ago. He willed his body to relax, behave and not embarrass them both. *Get it together, bro!*

"CANN International is one of the largest, most successful hotel developers in the world. Plus, with the urgency given to meeting as quickly as possible, I was curious and couldn't resist."

"Thank you for coming."

Once again Nick willed away the untimely musings and forced his thoughts more fully into the present. He motioned for Sam to have a seat in one of two chairs facing his desk, while he returned to his executive chair. A wide, paper-strewn desk created a physical barrier between them. Nick was appreciative of being reminded about this meeting's intent—all business, nothing personal. His body would do well to get the message, too.

He watched Sam place her briefcase on the floor, then sit back with squared shoulders. Professionalism oozed from her pores. Of course she wasn't daydreaming about that night long ago. She'd made time for the company and a possible job, not for him. Nick mentally chastised himself for the moment of weakness that had taken him down memory lane, and the discipline it took to rein in his body now. No matter that her hands were softer than he remembered, the designer suit failed to hide those dangerous curves, and the subtle scent that tickled his nose when he'd neared her for that handshake had made him want to pull her into an embrace. If the interview went well and Sam joined his team, they'd be working very closely together. Too close for a casual sexual dalliance. He'd do well to stay focused and remember that.

"Can I get you anything before we begin?"

"No, thank you," Sam replied. "I'm more than a little curious about what your assistant called an urgent matter but was unable to provide details."

"As I'd instructed," Nick said, leaning back in his chair. "I was equally intrigued with the news about you—that you were not only back in the States but here in Vegas and looking for clients."

Sam crossed her legs in one graceful, fluid motion with no idea, Nick assumed, of how utterly sexy a move it was.

"How did you hear? Probably someone from the function I recently attended," she continued before he could answer. "I did a great deal of networking to get the word out about the rebirth of Priceless Designs."

"Possibly." Nick shrugged. "It's a small town. News travels fast. Especially when your mother is Victoria Breedlove."

Sam smiled, this one genuine and relaxed. Her shoulders, tense and squared since entering his office, softened along with her face.

"How is your mother?"

"Still as nosy as she is wonderful."

"I don't know her personally, of course, but from everything I've read or heard about her she appears to have a great heart. That was evidenced at the luncheon, and the generous check presented to the Women in Business organization. I didn't see her, though. Someone else presented the check."

"Mom wasn't there. She and Dad have fallen in love with Scandinavia and since he's assured Mom his retirement is permanent, Dad has cloaked hotel location scouting missions under the guise of Nordic vacations. The girls stepped in to fill the gap left in her increasingly frequent absences."

"The girls?"

"Lauren, Ryan and Dee, my sisters-in-law, or in-love, as Mom always corrects me."

"Oh. Right."

"Their marriages were the wedding bells heard round the world. Surely you read about them."

Sam gave a slight shake of the head. "I'd heard about Christian's wedding but only learned that two more brothers had tied the knot upon returning to the States. How many brothers besides you does that leave standing single?"

"I stand alone," Nick dramatically intoned. "We have several business partners on the continent who said their nuptials made a big splash even there."

"While in Africa, I lived in a rather insular world."

"Since word on the street is you married a prince, a luxurious one, no doubt."

"Yes."

A physical wall couldn't have made Sam's intentions clearer. Whatever had happened while abroad, she didn't want to talk about it. But Nick couldn't resist.

"Yet you're back here and working. What does your husband think about that?"

"It doesn't matter. We're no longer together."

"Separated?"

"Divorced."

The tone beneath that one word closed the door on the subject of Sam's personal life better than King Tut's sealed tomb. It only made Nick even more curious, about both her failed marriage and her current love life. Now was obviously not the time to talk about it, but one day... Patience was not a virtue Nick knew well, but one he could employ when necessary. Now was definitely one of those times.

His body language remained relaxed but he adopted a businesslike tone. "Whatever brings you back to Las Vegas, your timing couldn't be better. I need the best and fastest-working designer that money can buy. Before running off to become an African princess, that was you."

A grin accompanied Sam's twinkling eyes. "I'd like to think it still is. What's going on?"

"A project that has to stay on schedule and a designer who isn't delivering on the promises she made."

"How many rooms are we talking about?"

"Not rooms...homes." Nick noted Sam's surprised expression. "This isn't a hotel design. It's a series of private island homes being advertised for vacation rental among the world's most elite."

"Wow. I had no idea you guys had expanded beyond the original hotel framework. Considering how the hospitality industry is changing, though, it sounds like a smart move."

"It's proven to be right on time with industry trends."

"Does that smirk confirm the obvious, that this was your idea?"

"Still a smart-ass, I see."

"Takes one to know one."

"Ha!"

"So I'm right."

"All of the brothers are involved but yes, it's more or less my baby. Which means failure is not an option. You feel me?"

"Tell me more."

Sam leaned forward, unconsciously revealing the slightest peek of a creamy quarter-moon of her breast. When his attention returned to her face, Sam was frowning. *Damn.* To her professional credit, however, she didn't comment on eyes determined to rove on their own. She simply adjusted her blouse and sat back, waiting, to learn why Nick had brought her here.

Nick leaned back as well, determined to take control of a meeting he'd called, ensconced in the comfort of discussing an industry he knew better than he knew himself. Business now, pleasure later, he thought as he began discussing his baby, CANN Isles. There was no way around it, even pushed to the back of his mind. The attraction for one Ms. Samantha "Sam" Price was real, intense and not going away.

Before it was mere speculation. Now she was sure. It shouldn't have mattered how much she wanted to see her old lover. Not only should Sam have not returned Anita's phone call, she shouldn't have made this appointment. She shouldn't be here with Nick. Her body was clear about it even if her mind wasn't sure. Every cell of her body had lit up, awakened by the irrefutable attraction that hadn't dimmed in all this time away. An attraction that given the sticky situation that even thinking of working with Nick presented, and the increasingly troublesome email and text exchanges with her ex, had no chance of being acted upon.

Being this close to him in proximity was TROUBLE, all caps. Just seeing him relax made her heart skip. She watched the lines on his forehead fade away as he broke into a spiel he'd probably recited a hundred times. Clearly, speaking about the company was his forte, his stomping grounds, his zone. But that brief look of desire she'd glimpsed before Nick realized he'd been caught staring at her cleavage suggested something impossible. That he still felt the attraction, too. Surely after all this time it was something she must have imagined. While the night she shared with Nick was seared into her conscience, and intimacy with her husband had been fleeting at best, she imagined there'd been a constant stream of women in and out of Nick's bedroom to make him forget all about it.

She wasn't quite sure when her attention went from what Nick was saying to the lips forming the words that came out of his mouth. But somewhere within his glib delivery about CANN International's latest expansion beyond casino hotels and spas into the lucrative and growing industry of offering private rental vacation homes, she was struck by the perfectly formed Cupid lips enunciating goals and intentions and reminding her of how skillfully they'd brought her to and over the orgasmic edge and changed her life forever. If her body was a violin, Nick's tongue was the bow that had played a melody etched in her soul, stamped into her mind and burned inside her heart. That night just over four years and nine short months ago when her world was rocked and shifted on its axis, was one she had no idea would be the catalyst for an adventure that took her from America to Africa and from fairy tale to nightmare, in less than five years.

"...Djibouti. Have you been there?"

Uh-oh. The uptick of his voice suggested to Sam that she'd just been asked a question. She had no idea what about.

"Um, not sure."

Wrong answer. Nick's frown told it all.

"Djibouti isn't the most popular of tourist destinations, but it is certainly memorable. Yet you're not sure?"

"No, I'm sure. I've never been there. Sorry, I got distracted. I silenced my phone but it's still vibrating." Sam reached into her purse. "I'll shut it off."

"Back less than a month and already in demand?"

"Something like that."

She quickly checked her text messages. It wasn't a slew of potential clients trying to reach her, but the very reason why she shouldn't be sitting there. Why as much as she wanted to, needed to, was desperate to, even, she couldn't take this job. No matter the pay, which she knew would be top-shelf.

Shooting off a quick reply, she then turned off the vibrating notifier and dropped the phone in the tote on the floor. "Sorry."

"No worries."

"You mentioned Djibouti. One of the islands CANN International owns is located there?"

Nick nodded. "Just off the coast on the Gulf of Aden. The first property built there is one of our smaller hotels, only eighty-nine rooms. All suites, though, with living and dining spaces, and spectacular ocean or mountain views. The casino is the building's jewel, of course, boasting a Michelin-star restaurant and world-class spa."

"I believe you guys are onto something. From all I've seen and understand, Africa's the next great economic frontier."

"That's what we believe, with Djibouti becoming the

next Dubai. It's why we're building more hotels all over the continent and have either purchased or designed a number of islands to house our luxury home rentals."

"So…you contacted me because you need someone based in Africa?"

"No. The projects needing immediate attention are mostly here in the US, along the eastern seaboard. But there are a couple in Hawaii and one in the Bahamas as well."

"All of this sounds amazing, Nick, but I don't yet understand the urgency or why I'm here."

"Because the designer we hired walked out. Last week. Couldn't keep pace with CANN's lofty vision, or take the pressures of a somewhat demanding boss—" Nick paused, Sam smiled "—and an increasingly tight deadline."

"What's happened to shrink the timeline?"

"Demand. The PR and marketing have been minimal but extremely targeted. Christian's wife, Lauren, designed the brochures and the job she did was outstanding. We knew they'd attract interest, but the response was far beyond what we'd planned. Instead of a slow rollout with an expected thirty to forty-five percent vacancy, almost eighty percent of the properties have already been booked. Including the ones that are not yet finished."

"That's impressive."

"And with the abrupt departure of our designer, problematic as well."

"So what you're saying is…the work she started on these homes needs to be finished?"

"Her work wasn't entirely up to our standards. You may be able to work your magic and salvage a few of the properties. Others will most likely need to be stripped and totally redone. Still more you'll have the pleasure of designing from the ground up. The homes were completed to the point of being an interior designer's blank canvas."

"Sounds major. How many homes are we talking?"

"Counting the properties in Hawaii and the Bahamas, twenty-three total."

Sam took a deep breath. That was a lot of designing, even for her. "And what's the desired completion date?"

Nick looked at his watch. "As of this morning…less than twelve weeks."

"Whoa!"

"Exactly. That's the urgency and why I called you."

"And why you didn't want your assistant to get into it."

"I didn't want you to get scared off before the entire scenario could be laid out. Because we know what a massive undertaking this is, and the immense pressure that will come from pulling it off, we're willing to compensate the designer who can handle the impossible with an equally unique offer."

Nick then laid out the compensation package, one so lucrative that not to accept would be stupid, insane, not even an option.

Still, she hesitated. "Can I think about it?"

"The employment package I've designed has never been offered to anyone," Nick responded. "Anywhere. Ever." Barely veiled frustration crept into his voice.

"No question the opportunity is amazing, but…"

A raised brow was Nick's only response.

"There are personal matters I'd need to consider, logistics that would have to be thought out."

"It's a phenomenal offer," Nick said, a slight frown marring his handsome face as he eyed her intently. "What's there to think about?"

"I have a son."

Crap! Did I say that out loud?

Nick's expression, subdued as it was, suggested that she had. The one thing she hadn't planned to share with Nick had just tumbled out before she could stop it.

"You have a child yet divorced the father? It's none of my business, but that had to be tough."

Sam nodded. It's all she could do.

"How old is he?"

"He's four," Sam replied, wishing the floor beneath her would turn to quicksand and swallow her whole.

"A boy, huh? I had no idea. Given all of the travel that's required, that adds a bit of a wrinkle that I didn't expect."

His eyes narrowed as he thoughtfully rubbed his chin. Sam could almost see his mind turning.

"We can add a childcare allowance to the package, work out an acceptable live-in arrangement so that your son's life isn't disrupted."

"That's an expensive suggestion and only a partial solution. Trey's life has already been upended with the move from Africa to America. I'm not sure how comfortable I'd be either leaving him with a virtual stranger or dragging him all over the States. I'd planned to put him in preschool for a bit of routine, stability. I don't know, Nick…"

"Given what I've just learned, I agree, Sam. It's a big ask. But I can't think of anyone who can do what needs to be done in the time that's required. Someone I trust. An award-winning, formerly sought-after designer whose skills I've seen firsthand.

"Listen, a large part of the charity my mom runs is geared toward helping children. Her network is filled with the best au pairs, teachers, tutors, childcare professionals, you name it. If you'd like, I can give you her number or have her call you. She can help you work something out, something beneficial for both you and… Trey, is it?" Sam nodded. "She can help with an arrangement in the best interest of both you and Trey. Don't let single motherhood be the reason you don't take the job."

Sam asked for a day to think about it, then left— translated, "escaped"—Nick's office. Accepting this meeting was a very bad idea, even worse than she imagined. Nick thought her having a child was the biggest challenge to working with him? No, the gargantuan one was that Nick was Trey's father…and didn't know it.

Two

"I didn't know Sam had a kid."

That was Nick's greeting later that day after walking into his twin brother Noah's house unannounced.

"Good afternoon to you, too, bro."

"You knew and didn't tell me?" Nick eyed Noah as he crossed the living room and plopped on the couch.

Noah shook his head. "No idea. How'd you find out?"

"During her interview for the design job."

"So you called her, huh? How'd that go?"

"Not as I'd planned. Because we need her like last week, I offered an employee package too generous for anyone to refuse. She asked for a day to think about it."

Nick laid out the package details.

Noah sat back, his look one of amazement. "What's there to think about?"

A lazy grin crept onto Nick's face. "That was my question exactly. And how I found out she'd become a mom."

Noah's phone pinged. He picked it up, tapped the face, then returned a quick text. He looked over at Nick. His expression changed. "How'd she look?"

"Sam? Better than the last time I saw her."

"The costume party, right?"

"Catwoman," Nick replied with a slow nod, allowing his mind for the briefest of moments to return to that night. Him, as a *GQ* Superman in a tight-fitting royal blue tux, red muscle shirt, and black-and-red mask. He'd been at the party for about an hour when he felt an energetic shift in the room. Samantha Price. The award-winning interior designer who'd flitted on the outskirts of his social circle for years. He flirted. She teased. As they'd always done. This time, though, he asked her to dance. After three minutes of slow dancing they left for CANN Casino Hotel and Spa, North America's only seven-star hotel and the jewel of Las Vegas. For the next twelve hours they stirred up enough electricity to light up the Strip. It was an unforgettable, mind-blowing night, when one sexy Catwoman became that Superman's kryptonite.

His twin, with whom he shared everything, was the only one he'd told.

Noah reached for his phone, viewed the lit-up screen. "You never saw her after that, right?"

"We were supposed to get together. But she left town, remember?"

"Vaguely."

"She met a prince and obviously started a family. Her body still looks amazing. I couldn't believe it when she told me she'd had a child."

"So the royal family is moving to America?"

Nick shook his head. "They're divorced."

"Sorry to hear that."

Nick nodded. That was an institution the Breedloves

didn't believe in. He probably should have felt sorry, too. But he didn't.

"How old is the kid?"

"Four."

"Boy or girl?"

"Boy. His name's Trey."

"What type of father would let his kid, especially a son, move to the other side of the world, divorce or no?"

"I thought the same thing. She clearly didn't want to talk about her personal life so I dropped the subject." Nick thoughtfully rubbed his five o'clock shadow, remembering the encounter. "She was different though, no doubt. Distant. Guarded. Not at all the carefree woman I remember."

"Having had to deal with whatever was bad enough to end her marriage, that can be understood. Maybe she was hoping they could have worked it out. Stayed together for the child's sake at least."

Noah's words reverberated. *Worked it out. Stayed together for the child's sake.* Nick didn't know how he felt about that.

"That design job is a beast with a time schedule from hell. I don't see her being able to do it. Not with a child."

"That definitely complicated the situation. Where there's a will, there's a way."

The room fell silent. Nick looked up to see Noah's speculative gaze.

"What?"

"Are you sure this is about getting the homes completed before summer?"

"Absolutely."

"It has nothing to do with Sam and the fact that she's single again?"

"Nothing."

"Liar."

They both laughed. "I'm focused on work, bro."

"I can understand that," Noah replied. "Plus, those Anderson twins are probably giving you all that you can handle."

"A gentleman never kisses and tells." Nick stood and headed toward the door.

Noah got up and walked toward him. "Where are you going?"

"I have a meeting."

"With whom?"

"The only person who can help me with the childcare dilemma." The brothers looked at each other and both said, "Mom."

Nick climbed into his flashy McLaren, sped down the road and spun into the circular driveway of his parents' estate in nothing flat.

"Mom!"

Helen, the housekeeper who after all of the decades she'd been employed there was more like an aunt, greeted him in the hallway. "Hello, Nick." The two shared a hug. "She's in her new favorite place."

"The solarium. Thanks, love."

Nick walked to the back of the home toward the newly added indoor/outdoor paradise that spanned a great length of the home. He walked over to where Victoria was engrossed in weeding a bed of vibrant plants. He sneaked up behind her and kissed her cheek.

"Oh!" Victoria swatted him. "You scared me!"

"Good thing I wasn't a burglar," he teased. "Did you have a chance to work on what I asked you or have you been here all morning, communing with nature?"

Victoria pulled off her gloves and set them on the rim of the wooden box before crossing over to a canvas-covered divan. "Your multitasking mother managed to do both." She poured a glass of lemon water and held up the pitcher.

"Please." She filled a glass for Nick and handed it to him. "Thanks."

"I ran across a picture of Sam online."

By "run across" Nick knew Victoria had scoured the internet to the edges of the earth to find out what she could about her.

"She's gorgeous, son. Those deep brown eyes. That flawless skin. Stunning."

"Yes, she's attractive."

"And married to a prince. Why is she back here and working, with a child to care for?"

"Those details aren't our business, Mom."

"I was just curious. I'd imagine her child is equally beautiful. Does he look like her?"

"How would I know?"

"She didn't show you a picture?"

"It was an interview, Mom, not a social visit."

"Still, son, it's a rare mother who doesn't offer up pictures of her children at the slightest opportunity."

It would be even rarer if one such mother didn't begin another round of internet sleuthing to find one.

"Any success on finding contacts I can pass on to Sam?"

"I've asked Hazel to pull together a list of possibilities."

"Your new assistant?" Victoria nodded. "How is she working out?"

"No one will ever top Lauren's skills, but Hazel is a close second. She'll compile a list of names and agencies and forward them to you by end of day."

"You're amazing."

"I try."

Nick stood. Victoria followed suit.

"I've got more work to do." He kissed her forehead and pulled her in for a hug. "You're a lifesaver, Mom. Thanks."

"Keep me posted on how it all goes."

"I will. Love you, Mom."

"Love you more."

Nick returned to his car and immediately called Sam. It would have made more sense to wait until he'd received the list, but he wanted to hear her voice now.

"Hello?" Sam sounded breathless, liked she'd rushed to the phone. A thought flashed about another time when heavy breathing occurred, but he immediately shut it down.

"Sam. Nick."

"Hey, Nick."

"Good news. I'm about to solve all your problems."

"You know them all?"

Nick laughed. "You have that many?"

"A few." No laughter. "Is this about the job? You said I had until tomorrow, right? I still haven't made up my mind."

"If part of the indecision is about childcare, a solution is on the way."

"It is?"

"Yep."

"So…let me guess. In addition to being a vice president in a multibillion-dollar corporation, you own a childcare center?"

"No, but I know…hey. What are you doing?"

"Right now?"

"Yes, right now."

"On the computer, research stuff. There's a lot to do to get settled."

"I bet. Where are you staying?"

"South Vegas, temporarily."

"I'm headed that way. Let's discuss the childcare solution I've come up with over dinner."

"I can't do that. I need to get dinner for…for my son."

"That's no problem. Bring the little guy, too. I know a kid-friendly spot not far from our hotel. You and Trey can meet me there." Silence fell as Noah exited the freeway and headed toward CANN Casino Hotel and Spa, a towering landmark anchoring one end of the Las Vegas Strip. "Sam, you there?"

"Yeah, um, I'm here. Thanks, but no. I'm going to run us through a drive-through and get right back online. What's the name of the daycare center? I'll check out their website."

"All of your options are being compiled. I'll have them later today. With the long hours and frequent travel, the list will most likely include au pairs or child assistants with degrees in child education. That way if Trey travels with you, he'll still stay on course with his preschool studies. I think the best candidate would be someone who can look after Trey and whatever temporary households you establish wherever you're at."

"Sounds awesome, Nick, but even with your company's amazing offer, I'm not sure I could afford an arrangement like that. Her salary, airfare, extra lodging, food. It would be a huge expense."

"You're right. I thought about that, which is why her employment would be a part of your package. She'll be employed by the company and, like you, would be given a company card for travel and other expenses."

"Wow. This is… I'm speechless. Where would you find such a person? How…"

"Mom. Plain and simple. She's a better problem-solver and negotiator than a top corporate exec, including my father. Including me. The people on the list have been pre-vetted and most likely were recommended by someone Mom personally knows."

"I… I don't know what to say."

"That's easy. Say you'll be by my office tomorrow to complete the paperwork. You can meet the au pair, sit with our real estate executive to help you with housing and get ready for a trip to New York next week."

"Whoa, Nick, slow down. You're throwing a lot at me. It's almost too much."

"You can handle it."

"I appreciate your confidence but with all of the amazing designers out there, why are you doing all of this to get me?"

"That's simple, Sam. Because you're the best."

"How can I argue with that?"

"You can't."

Why did Sam's laughter make Nick feel like beating his chest and unable to wipe the grin off his face?

"I don't know, Nick. This is a lot to think about."

"You still have a few hours. Why don't you stop by the office tomorrow, say three o'clock?"

"Okay."

"See you then. And Sam?"

"Yes?"

"Just so you know. When I see you tomorrow, the only acceptable answer to my job offer is yes."

Three

Sam reached the hall at one end of the living room, turned and retraced her steps back to the fireplace on the opposite wall. She'd paced this way for the past fifteen minutes. Talking with her cousin, the one who'd graciously taken in her and Trey after their abrupt stateside return. Making her case.

"I can't take this job, Danni. There's no way!"

"There's no way you cannot take it. That job is everything you need right now. With childcare included? Girl, please."

"This isn't about the money. It's about…" Sam looked toward the hallway where her son shared a room with his cousin. She went to sit by Danielle and lowered her voice. "This is about Trey. I can't imagine what would happen if Nick ever found out."

"He's Trey's father, Sam." Danni's voice was a whisper as well. "He shouldn't have to find out. He should be told. The sooner the better."

Sam understood what was behind that last statement. Her ex, Oba, what he knew and how he could use the information if things turned ugly.

Danielle reached out and placed a hand on Sam's arm. "As much as you wanted to deny it, cousin, you knew this day would come. I told you it would."

Sam stared at the fireplace, feeling tears threaten. She watched flames dance and felt a personal inferno.

"It all happened so fast. I was so scared back then. Your friend Joi called. We talked. She gave her brother my number. Oba reached out, then flew over. The next thing I knew I was saying I do. An admittedly hasty arrangement that at the time seemed to solve both his and my problems. I thought leaving without telling Nick was best for everyone. I planned to keep the secret for the rest of my life."

"I know. I'm not blaming or judging you for your choices. If anything, I feel partly responsible. I hate that I shared what Joi told me about her brother looking for a marriage of convenience to beat their egotistical brother to the throne."

"Don't blame yourself. I jumped at the chance. Knowing how Nick felt about marriage, let alone children, made Oba's proposal seem like a magical solution. That I was pregnant gave me an advantage over the other possible candidates. At the time it seemed like a win-win for everyone."

Sam thought back to the morning after she and Nick had been together. How he'd questioned her about birth control, asked if she was protected. She told him yes because she'd been absolutely sure at that time that she could not get pregnant. A problem with fibroids that she'd had for years. He'd worn condoms from then on, two more rounds before leaving the suite that afternoon. All except for that wild, hedonistic, incredible first romp when Trey was created.

"You did the best that you could at the time. But when we know better, we do better."

Now it was Danielle who stood and began walking a hole in the rug. "This is all my fault, really."

Sam looked up. "Did you not hear a word of what I just said?"

"I heard you, Sam. If I'd never heard about the prince or told Joi you were pregnant…"

"As a wise person just told me, you did what you thought was best at the time. When we know better, we do better."

Danielle returned to the sofa. "What's the best decision now? Not just for you but for Trey, even Nick? It doesn't seem right that your ex-husband knows he's not Trey's father but Nick doesn't know that he is. I know that's advice you didn't ask for but…"

"No, you're right. I can't keep the secret forever. Nick deserves to know that he is a father and Trey needs to grow up with his dad."

"Does Trey ask about Oba?"

Sam shook her head. "Trey was always a means to an end for him. He wasn't harsh or anything—they had playful interactions. But Oba isn't overly affectionate and was never hands-on. He also felt child-rearing was 'the woman's job.'" Sam used air quotes, and made a face. "Plus, he was always gone, handling royal business, or jet-setting all over the world."

"From everything you've told me about Nick's offer, sounds like you'll be the one jet-setting now."

"For sure. Designing luxury homes on beautiful islands with an unlimited budget would be a job beyond my wildest dreams." Sam sighed, rested her head on the back of the couch. "But how can I work with Nick and not tell him about Trey? And once that happens, how could he hire me or, if I've taken the job, keep me on?"

"All good questions," Danielle said, as she stood to leave the room. "And only one way to find out."

Sam had just gone to bed when her phone pinged. She checked the text. Oba. Again. Danielle was right. She needed to tell Nick about Trey. But with her mother's cancer battle draining Sam's savings, and the rest used to flee Africa for the safety of home, she also desperately needed the job.

Sam got little sleep that night. She was grateful that Danielle had made arrangements for Trey to join his cousins at day care again. Her husband, Scott, left just before Danielle and the kids. Sam found a yoga video online, one that focused on specific postures and deep breathing. For an hour she worked to think about nothing at all and was mostly successful. As soon as the last chime on the video sounded, however, it was like all of the thoughts and questions she'd held at bay during the workout rushed in at once.

Would Nick be angry?

Would he consider giving a job to someone who lied by omission, one he'd almost surely not trust?

Would the powerful Breedloves fight to take her child?

Could she support her son financially without them?

Sam took a shower, then walked to her closet to dress for success. From the time she was young her mother told her, "When you look good, you feel good." It was a lesson Sam never forgot. She flipped through the meager wardrobe she'd packed and considered a well-fitting yet respectable red dress with long sleeves and a scoop neck.

She remembered yesterday's meeting, and how Nick's eyes had slid to her legs when she crossed them, his surreptitious glance when she'd shifted in the chair and her blouse played peekaboo. It had taken everything to act as though she hadn't noticed. Or that muscle memory from their single rendezvous hadn't kicked in, and caused her to clench and harden in places that should he become her boss would be totally off-limits. His charm drove her crazy and he was still as fine as forbidden fruit. But the only thing more out of the question than whether or not she should work with Nick was whether to sleep with him. That answer was a big fat irrefutable *no*.

When she pulled into CANN Casino Hotel and Spa's valet parking, Sam still hadn't made up her mind. Time had run out before the right answer revealed itself. She entered the building, retraced her steps from the day before and decided to go with the flow. While walking through the opulent lobby, with its contemporary motif of marble, stainless steel and crystal chandeliers, her phone rang. She almost didn't answer it. But it could be about Trey.

"Sam Price."

"Hey, it's Nick."

"Am I late? I'm in the lobby and—"

"No, you're not late. I'm hungry. I hope you don't mind that I've moved our meeting to Zest, one of our restaurants. Just get on one of the upper-floor elevators. It's got its own button."

"Oh, okay. I'm on my way." Before having time to process this change of events, the sleek, fast elevator had whisked her far above the bustling metropolis below and landed her into the kind of luxury she came to enjoy as the princess of Kabata, the province her ex-husband Oba and his family had ruled for several generations. Her heartbeat quickened in anticipation.

"Good afternoon. Welcome to Zest."

"Hi, I'm Sam. Samantha Price. I'm here to meet—"

"We've been expecting you, Ms. Price," the hostess said, with sparkling blue eyes and a genuine smile. "Please, come right this way."

Sam took in the floor-to-ceiling paneless glass that blended the clear blue sky with the room's similarly painted ceilings and expected to be escorted into the dining area. Instead, they went along the outer hall of the smartly appointed main dining room to a series of doors along the dimly lit corridor. The hostess stopped in front of the first door on the left, tapped lightly and opened it.

"Mr. Breedlove, Ms. Price has arrived." She stepped back to allow Sam to enter the room. "Enjoy your meal."

Sam thought she'd do better at seeing Nick this time, since she'd just seen him hours before. But his handsomeness still unnerved her. His gentlemanly action of standing as she entered warmed her insides. What guy did that these days? The way his eyes swept her body touched her to the core, brought back feelings from that one single night as though it had just happened. Which was why in that moment she knew their one-night stand was the first thing they needed to discuss.

"Hello, Nick," she said, holding out a stiff arm. A firm handshake was all of this man's touch she could handle.

"Sam, good to see you." He motioned to a chair. "Please, have a seat. I hope you don't mind that I moved our meeting. I've been here working since before seven this morning. It wasn't until Anita reminded me of our meeting that I realized I hadn't eaten all day."

"It's no problem at all."

"Are you sure?"

Sam knew why he asked. She was acting strangely, not like herself. If she was going to work with him, a possibility that was not yet decided, she'd have to pull it together.

"Positive," she managed, trying to relax as she spoke.

"Are you hungry?"

"I'm fine."

"I know that," Nick said with a mischievous grin. "You're still as beautiful as ever. But would you like something to eat?"

Sam refused to be distracted by Nick's limitless charisma. "I'm not hungry, thanks."

"I hope that wasn't offensive."

Sam looked away from his unflinching gaze, deep chocolate orbs framed by curly black lashes. That's how the dance that started at the party all those years ago had ended up in a luxury suite. She'd gotten lost in those eyes.

Nick continued. "In this post-#MeToo world, we male execs have to be extra careful. But given our past friendship, well, I hope complimenting you wasn't uncomfortable. I meant no disrespect."

"No worries."

A second later, there was a knock at the door. A white-haired server entered with a rolling tray containing glasses and a pitcher filled with pomegranate iced tea.

"May I recommend the chateaubriand today, sir? It is exceptional."

Nick looked across the table. "Sam?"

"Nothing for me, thanks."

The server looked at Nick. "I'll take the chateau, Fredrich," he said, resting against the high-backed leather chair.

"Excellent choice," Fredrich replied as he poured two glasses of tea. "The tenderloin comes from an award-winning ranch not far from here." Fredrich winked at Nick, then looked at Sam.

"If I may," Fredrich began with a benevolent smile. "May I have the pleasure of choosing something for you, something light, or a smaller dish if you prefer?"

"The beef is from my brother Adam's ranch," Nick added. "It's some of the best in the country. Plus, I'm buying, and this place has a Michelin star."

When Sam hesitated, Nick continued. "Come on, woman. It's not wise to turn down a fancy free meal."

The server looked so hopeful Sam couldn't refuse. "Sure," she said, blessing him with a smile. "Thanks."

Fredrich gave a short bow and left.

"Good choice. You won't be sorry." Nick raised a glass. "To a productive meeting."

Sam wasn't so sure about how productive it would be. But she raised a delicately chiseled crystal goblet, clinked it against Nick's and said, "Cheers."

"I know twenty-four hours wasn't a long time to make this decision, but I hope you've had time to think about the benefits of accepting our offer."

"It's all I've thought about," Sam honestly responded. "But before we talk about the job offer, there's something else we need to address."

Nick reached for his glass and sat back. "Oh?"

"That night the last time we saw each other. I don't know about you but for me, it's the elephant in the room."

"If memory serves me correctly, I believe it was a cat."

Nick smiled. Sam didn't.

"I need to make sure that what happened years ago has no bearing on our potential relationship now. If I decide to work for CANN International, the interaction between you and me must be strictly professional. Nothing else."

Nick gave her a look. "Of course."

It was the exact answer Sam wanted, but did he have to reply so quickly? As if the thought of a rekindled affair, even briefly, had not even crossed his mind?

Four

Nick was taken aback by Sam's statement but like the great amateur poker player he was, he didn't let that fact show on his face. Sam had just laid out in no uncertain terms the boundaries of their relationship. Hers was a wise choice, the only one really, especially given the time crunch they'd be under. What else was there to say?

"I didn't mean to imply that you… I just didn't want to assume anything. I wanted to be very clear that this is a business relationship."

"A business relationship? Does that mean you're giving serious consideration to the job offer?"

"I'd be crazy not to," Sam admitted. "Especially since you offered to assist with childcare, which was a major concern, and probably the number one challenge to me accepting the offer."

Number two, she inwardly corrected herself. Her secret about Trey was numero uno.

"If that issue is resolved, you'll take the job?"

"You've made it a very difficult offer to turn down. If it was just me to consider, the decision would be easier. But I have to think of my son. As I said yesterday, he's had what was a very stable world turned upside down. He's been relocated across continents and removed from almost all of the people he knows."

"I can't imagine." Nick's eyes conveyed the compassion he felt. "You a newly single mom. His dad now so far away."

Or not, Sam thought, but said nothing.

"Listen, Sam. CANN International, this project, means a great deal to me, but family is everything. I wouldn't want to do anything to compromise the well-being of your son. It's why throwing in the benefits of an au pair plus was a no-brainer. Both Christian and Adam swear that their assistants are invaluable, like part of the family."

"That's who helped compile the list of childcare options you sent over, your brothers?"

"I talked to them, but Mom and her assistant Hazel made the list. She thinks live-in help who can also provide tutoring would be the best type of aide for your situation. Isabella and Kirtu, the young women who work for my brothers, are very important components in the smooth running of their households. Given what you've just told me about Trey, I know that familiarity and routine are extremely important right now."

Sam nodded. Was it her imagination or did a softness enter Nick's voice when he said his son's name?

"I think Trey having another constant in his life, someone who'd be there no matter where you're working or what the hours, would be a good thing."

"What happens when the job is over?"

"Good question, though one you might not have to confront right away. CANN International is a huge corporation. Lots of properties to decorate and stage. I could see you being a part of it for the long haul."

"That's what I thought about my marriage," Sam mumbled.

Nick rarely squirmed. At this comment, however, he shifted in his seat. "I'm sorry."

"No, it's not you. It's me. There's a lot going on. I would like to explore working with CANN but honestly, Nick, I'm in no shape to make long-term decisions right now."

"Fair enough. We could bring you on as a contractor and if it works out, look at something more permanent later on. Would that work?"

Sam hesitated before nodding her head. "It sounds like a great opportunity. I'd love to take you up on it."

Nick felt his shoulders relax. Until that moment of relief, he hadn't realized how badly he wanted to hear some type of yes in her response.

"Good answer." The door opened. Nick looked up as Fredrich entered behind a rolling tray. "And perfect timing."

Fredrich placed a bread basket in the center of the table, along with a carousel of butters and jams. Nick reached for the butter knife with one hand and a biscuit with the other.

"These are legendary," he began, spreading a lavish amount of herbed butter on the still-warm bun. "Made fresh daily, as are all of the bakery items. Come on, you've got to try one."

"I have to admit that the smell coming from beneath that cloth is amazing." She lifted the linen, perused the assortment of mini-treats and picked up a roll. She sniffed. "Parmesan."

Nick paused to watch her. She closed her eyes and took a bite. Despite his determination to keep their relationship professional, the look of pure bliss on her face reminded him of a different type of nibbling they'd enjoyed one other time.

"These should be illegal," she said after finishing the roll.

"I told you," Nick said, with a laugh. "Bon appétit."

They spent the next several minutes discussing specifics of the contract. Fredrich returned with a medium-rare delight for Nick and an exquisite chopped salad topped with velvety slices of chateaubriand for Sam. Conversation was momentarily paused as Nick dug into his roasted vegetables and Sam poured a tangy vinaigrette over her fare.

After a few bites, she put down her fork and picked up her napkin. "I had some amazing meals while living in the palace. But I never knew a simple salad could taste like this."

"I wouldn't use that word in front of the chef. He'd probably say there's nothing simple about it."

Sam took another bite of the delectable combination of brussels sprouts, kale, sweet onion and beef, drizzled with the sweet tangy dressing and sprinkled with a finely grated cheese. She closed her eyes, chewed slowly and moaned.

Nick's dick jumped. *Down, boy.* Memories best forgotten threatened to derail his thought process again.

Sam opened her eyes. "You're right. It looks that way. So few ingredients. But the depth of flavor…"

"Sounds like you know your way around a kitchen."

"Not at all. My cousin does, though. Cooking shows are her obsession."

"The cousin you were with at the party that night?"

"Yes. Wow. I'm surprised you remembered."

It was a memorable night. "What's her name?"

"Danielle. We call her Danni."

Nick nodded, thinking back to the pillow talk they'd enjoyed in between sexual romps. Sam and Danni. Boy names for the bad-boy toys. Those had been her words that night. He kept that memory to himself. When Sam quickly changed the subject, he followed her lead.

"How did your family get into the vacation home rental business?"

Nick finished a bite of food. "By accident."

"And now you've got houses all over the world? Some accident."

"It's the truth." Nick shrugged. "At least the short version."

"What's the longer one?"

Nick finished his plate and sat back with his drink. "It started with my oldest brother, Christian, who built the hotel off the coast in Djibouti. Around that same time, I had business on an island off the coast of New York."

"The property you now own?"

"Yes. It is close to the city yet completely private and already had what we needed in place—utilities, roads. It's small, not large enough for a hotel but perfect for smaller homes. After securing that property, and as research continued, we purchased islands off the coasts of North and South Carolina, Georgia, California and Maine. All of this information will be in your sign-on packet and goes into deeper detail. Next week, you'll see it firsthand."

"Hotels, homes and islands, too? CANN International is bigger than I thought."

"Which is why coming on board to work with us is the best decision you could have ever made."

"With your biased opinion I think it best that I be the judge of that."

"Ha! Touché."

The conversation continued, becoming lighter and more organic as Sam continued to loosen up. By the time Fredrich removed the dessert dishes and poured the black coffee he'd suggested as their digestif, the easy camaraderie from that past casual encounter had returned. Nick felt even better about his decision to reach out to Sam. Not only was she the best woman for a job of this magnitude, she could be a lot of fun.

"Thanks for talking me into eating," Sam said as they stood. "I didn't think I was hungry until I took the first bite."

"Breedloves take food seriously," Nick joked. "We put as much thought into hiring chefs as we do floor designs."

They stepped out of the private dining room and continued down the hall that ran alongside the main dining area. Workers scurried from table to table, making each a perfect presentation for the dinner crowd. Nick acknowledged a few of them as they passed by, left the restaurant and headed toward the elevator.

Nick pressed the button and stepped back. "I'll have paperwork drawn up and faxed over ASAP. You have a passport, obviously, so we don't have to worry about that."

"Passport? Aren't all of the builds for this project happening stateside?"

"The last home we'll renovate is in the Bahamas. Other than that, international travel will most likely not be required. We make sure everyone working for us has the paperwork required to travel to any number of our CANN properties, just in case."

The elevator arrived. They stepped inside, both quiet during the ride down one hundred floors.

Once in the lobby, Nick held out his hand. "Welcome aboard, Ms. Price."

"Those papers aren't signed yet, Mr. Breedlove." Sam teased. "But I don't foresee any problems."

She accepted his handshake. Her skin was warm, velvety soft to the touch. Their eyes met. Something happened between them. Faint, but perceptible. A current of erotic energy sparkled in their midst. Sam pulled her hand from Nick's grasp. The spell was broken. But Nick had definitely felt it and was 99.9 percent sure that Sam had felt it, too.

They said goodbye and went their separate ways. Yet long after their meeting and into the night, Nick wondered about the elephant that Sam had brought up. It wasn't that lone, torrid night of the past that he was worried about. It was the undeniable chemistry still sizzling between them, and how long it could be successfully ignored.

Five

There were a few showers when April arrived, but for most Nevadians the warmer breezes were a welcome change from the previous month's unseasonably cold temperatures. Sam barely noticed. After signing the project-specific contract and faxing it back to CANN International, the next eight days passed in a whirlwind— a flurry of house hunting and childcare interviews. She ignored Nick's suggestion to move to Breedlove, an unincorporated area not far from Las Vegas, but accepted the born-and-bred native's advice on the best areas in Las Vegas to rent. She also politely declined the company's offer to assist with her search for a nanny. Telling Nick the truth about Trey was inevitable. But until she was ready and the time was right, Sam planned to keep the Breedloves and CANN International far away from her child. After last night's conversation with Oba, she was thankful that an ocean separated them, too. She couldn't believe he'd had the nerve to call.

* * *

"Oba?"

"You forget my voice already, baby?"

Sam didn't have to work to give her ex the silent treatment. She literally had nothing to say.

"How is life in America?"

Really? He was treating this as a social call? After how their relationship ended, and all that had happened since then?

"Oba, I'm busy, on my way to begin a very important project. I can't talk now."

"A working woman? Oh, no, *masoyina*! That is not the life for you."

"I am no longer your love, your wife or your responsibility. I thought we agreed a clean, complete break was best. Why are you calling me?"

"I miss you, baby. I miss my son."

The endearment was spoken with a low and heartfelt intonation, an emphasis on the second syllable, as was his way. The same voice she at one time appreciated now brought knots to her stomach. Oba had given Trey only a passing interest. What was this really about? That the marriage was one of convenience had been something they'd both willingly entered and ended. He needed to let it go.

"Last week, my father delivered very bad news, baby. He is still very angry at our deception."

Our deception?

"That he welcomed Trey into the family with a ceremonial tribute reserved for only those with tribal blood."

And this is my business because...

"I'm sorry that your father is unhappy, Oba. But his learning about Trey not being your son isn't my fault. That was your brother's doing. We've both suffered because of the decision Isaac made. I lost a lot, including the little money I'd been able to save while living there. I'm doing what I have to do to rebuild my life and am not sure how what is happening within your family involves me."

"My father has severely limited my royal responsibilities and by extension, my allowance."

"At least you have one."

"It is not how I am accustomed to living. He has banished me to the apartment in Lagos, a place I've only stayed in sporadically and not for several years!"

Sam visited that apartment once. It was a two-story unit with four bedrooms, five bathrooms, a tennis court and a pool. Poor baby.

"Oba, what do you want from me?"

"I need to make some moves, Sam. Maybe come to America."

"You've got Joi here. Ask her for help."

"She doesn't have any money."

"I don't either," Sam quickly retorted.

"But you can get it." Oba's tone changed, became firmer and a little less friendly. "Ask Nick to give it to you."

"What?" Sam's voice rose several octaves. That after several shocked seconds before she could actually speak, the nerve and unmitigated gall of his suggestion rendering her paralyzed and dang near mute.

She sat straight up in bed. "Are you freaking kidding me? Are you out of your mind? I don't have any money to give you and asking Nick or anyone else for help is out of the question."

"Does he know about Trey?"

"Keep Trey out of this."

"That sounds like a no."

"I don't give a damn how it sounds or what you think you know about Trey's relationship with his biological father."

Sam hoped that sentence was enough of a dam to stop the potential flood of truth hinted at by Oba's veiled threat.

"Trey is the innocent party in all of this and totally off-limits. As for what's happened because of your brother, well, we've both suffered from his actions. If anyone can and should help you it's Isaac, not me. And definitely not Nick."

"You know I'm the last person with whom Isaac would share his wealth. I helped you out when you were in trouble. Now you need to return the favor."

"How many ways do I have to say it? I don't have any money."

"According to my sister, that's about to change. She sent me a link to a press release. You're working with CANN International."

Sam hadn't given a thought to making news, would not have believed the hiring of a contractor warranted a public announcement. Damn the company and their PR efficiency, and damn Joi for not minding her business.

"It's a temporary contract," she replied, then quickly searched the web for the announcement, and hoped the verbiage didn't go into detail.

It didn't, thank God. But Oba already knew too much.

"My getting work doesn't change the answer. There is nothing I can do to help you."

"Listen, Sam—"

"No, you listen. I'm done talking." Sam stopped, took a breath, removed the crease from between her brows and calmed down. Offending Oba right now would do her no good. "I wish you the best, Oba, and hold nothing against you. But because of Isaac, we are out of each other's lives. Let's continue to move on, going separate ways. We're both doing our best under the circumstances. Please don't call me again."

Sam arrived at the airport in Las Vegas for a flight to New York. She reached the gate and looked for Nick. He wasn't there. The boarding announcement sounded over the speakers. Still, no Nick. She pulled out her cell to call him but changed her mind. He wasn't her responsibility. Maybe he'd decided not to accompany her. No big deal. She was an accomplished designer who didn't require hand-holding. That he'd planned to come at all had been a surprise in the first place. Sam had a first-class ticket but waited until several had boarded before getting on the plane. After accepting an orange juice from the attendant, she settled in for the flight, convinced she'd hear from Nick after landing in New York. Instead, just before the doors closed, he rushed in and took the aisle seat beside her.

"Hey," he said, passing off his briefcase and buckling his seat belt in a rush.

"Cutting it a bit close, aren't we?"

"Didn't mean to. Saw a buddy of mine in the lounge and got to talking. Lost track of time."

"It's all good. You made it. Considering the success of the company you work for I'm surprised you fly commercial at all."

"I don't often," Nick admitted.

"I hope you didn't lower your standards on my account." Sam smiled to show she was joking. She was. In a way.

"I'd hardly call spending time with you in any way lowering my standards," Nick easily replied, his voice lower than usual and sexier than Sam would have liked. "Plus, with it being so long since we've seen each other I thought the long nonstop flight would be a perfect chance to catch up.

"So…" he continued, after casually chatting while the plane reached its cruising altitude. "Tell me about living the life of a princess."

It was a fair question, one Sam might have asked were the situation reversed. She shifted in her seat. "Well, as Meghan Markle would probably attest, it's not always all it's cracked up to be. But it wasn't all bad."

"How'd you meet Oba Usman, the grand prince of Kabata and rumored heir to the throne?"

"Someone's been busy online, I see." Said as Sam prided the exterior she managed, one that masked the angst she felt just beneath the surface. Given what had happened that caused Oba to lose his right to the throne, the less Nick knew about her ex, the better.

"A little background research on our latest corporate partner. This would have normally been all done beforehand had I not been under the gun to hire someone so quickly."

Sam couldn't fault him for researching her via web. She'd done the same to him after meeting that night at the party. It's where she first learned he was a successful confirmed bachelor who didn't want kids.

"Danni, who you remember from the party, was friends with his sister. Shortly after meeting me she talked to him. Thought we might make a good match. We were introduced via a video chat and it went from there."

"Interesting. Things must have moved fast. I mean, one minute we're hanging out at a costume party and the next you're married and living on the other side of the world."

"Yes, everything happened quickly." For reasons that remained unsaid. "I admit to moving forward with stars in my eyes. Every little girl dreams of being a princess, and fantasizes about knights in shining armor once we reach our teens."

"And Oba seemed to be that?"

"I thought so, in the beginning."

"What changed?"

Sam took a deep breath and spoke thoughtfully. "I've come to realize that even under the most normal of circumstances, marriage is hard. That mine was high-profile and involved a royal family added to the challenge."

Nick whistled. "Going through that had to be tough. One of the main reasons I'm in no hurry to do it."

"Smart move."

"Why'd you marry so quickly?"

"Oba was under pressure to find a wife. Being married and producing an heir was a requirement for him to be considered as a successor to the throne, something his younger brother who'd become engaged the year prior was in a race to do. When… I became pregnant…we married right away."

"Was it what you wanted?"

Sam avoided looking into Nick's penetrating gaze. "It's what I felt best for Trey."

"And for you?"

"At the time I thought the decision best for the both of us."

"Hmm. How is the little guy? Did you find a suitable nanny?"

"I think so. For now, Danni is graciously handling everything between Gloria, the nanny, and Trey. I'll fly them up later, probably next week."

As the flight attendant began the first-class meal service, Sam and Nick retreated to their individual thoughts. Sam was relieved for the reprieve, a time to recover from the stress felt during that conversation. She replayed and mentally tucked away what had been said, in order to make sure that the story she told now, in this moment, was one she'd remember if ever asked again.

"What about you? I know you're in no hurry but with all of your brothers married, you're not feeling the slightest pressure to walk down the aisle, have a kid or two, and contribute to the Breedlove legacy?"

Nick stretched his long, lean legs in front of him. "Not at all."

Sam couldn't help but laugh at the hasty response, even as Nick not being ready to have children made her heart skitter around in her chest.

Nick positioned his chair to lean back. "For now, these island homes are my only babies. It's the biggest company project I've taken on to date, and while the family hasn't applied any pressure, I have my own point to prove.

"In the past few years," he continued, counting on his fingers, "Christian's build in Djibouti opened up the entire African continent. Adam's Wagyu beef is the best in America, and with his land research and development gem finds he's contributed greatly to the company's bottom line. Last year Noah did the impossible by opening up a casino in what is arguably the country's most conservative state. While paralyzed."

Sam gasped. "Oh no! What happened?"

"Horrific ski accident. You didn't hear?" Sam shook her head. "Wow, you really were isolated."

"Mostly by choice. Before, my phone and the internet were like an extension of my physical self. It was nice to step away from all that and live in the real world, such as it was."

"I can't imagine, but I hear you."

"How is Noah now?"

"Much better, thanks for asking."

"Sounds like the past few years have been very productive for the family. Now it's your turn?"

"Yes."

"Do they have kids, your brothers?"

Nick nodded. "Christian has a daughter, Christina, and a son, Larenz. Both Adam's and Noah's wives, Ryan and Dee, are expecting. They conceived three months apart."

"Wow! Sounds like Uncle Nick is going to be busy."

"Yeah, being the uncle is great. I can be the fun adult, spoil them and then send them home."

They laughed, and the conversation paused as the flight attendant returned with menus. She'd been flirting with Nick since he sat on the plane and now was no exception.

"Mr. Breedlove, may I recommend the salmon." She paused, batting long lashes and flashing flawless pearly whites as she refreshed his drink. "It's really good and healthy, too. You seem the type who likes to stay in shape."

"You're right about that." He handed back the menu. "I'll have that with asparagus and rice."

"Great choice." She looked at Sam. "And for you?" Asked with no sparkling eyes, a mere hint of a smile and no move to freshen her drink.

Sam almost laughed out loud. "I'll have the Cajun chicken salad, please. And a glass of cabernet."

Both of them watched the attendant walk away.

Sam nodded in her direction. "Looks like you have an admirer."

"She's just doing her job."

"Seriously, Nick, you can't be that naive. Your modesty, though, is appreciated."

He took a sip of water. "Tell me about your family. Do you have siblings?"

"A brother from my mom's first marriage. He's seven years older than me, a techie who lives in Seattle. My dad lives in LA."

"Is that where you grew up?"

"Born and raised."

"And your mom?"

Sam quieted, swallowed past the sudden lump in her throat. "She passed away right before I moved to Africa. Breast cancer."

"I'm sorry."

"Thank you. I miss her every day."

"How is it that you were at the costume party?"

Sam knew exactly which party he was talking about, the one where they slept together and her life was forever changed.

"Danni moved here years ago, a professional dancer with stars in her eyes. Got hired for a few shows. Then she met Scott, got married and started a family. Her mom, my aunt, was my mom's sister. They were very close, always together, which led to Danni and I being more like sisters than cousins."

"What did she think about your quick wedding?"

Back to that again? Sam wondered why Nick was so fixated on a marriage that was over. She chose to answer rather than ask the question; figured the more open she was about that part of her life the less he'd feel the need to pry further.

"She's always wanted what was best for me. Since I was happy, she was happy."

"And now that you're divorced?"

Sam tried not to let her chagrin show but she had tired of this line of questioning. "Again, she supports whatever is best for me, and is happy I'm back stateside."

"Please forgive my insensitivity for asking. I imagine that ending a marriage is never easy, no matter the reason, and that talking about it could be painful."

"You're right. It's not easy. But in the end, it was for the best. Enough about me. Let's talk about your love life."

"I already told you. The only love affair I'm having right now is with the CANN Isles project."

"If that's your story you can stick to it. But an architect's art renderings can't keep you warm at night."

"Ha! True that. I go out here and there but mostly I've been too busy to date."

Sam found that hard to believe but didn't push. The conversation wound its way back to business and the cluster of island homes in New York, the first that Sam would be stamping with her designs. Were circumstances different she'd definitely date Nick. Smart and confident with a wicked sense of humor, he wasn't hard to like. That he was easy on the eyes didn't hurt, either. Being far and away the best lover she'd ever experienced would be the cherry on top of the sundae. If things were different. But they weren't. Sam needed to keep that in mind and stay focused on doing her job.

The flight attendant returned. The flirting continued. Sam put on a brave smile and hid the anguish in her heart. The best thing that could happen was for Nick to fall madly in love, thereby erasing any perceived chance of a future between them. She, Trey and Nick would not ride off into the sunset as one big happy family. Whatever feelings that were trying to resurface were best quashed before having a chance to blossom.

No doubt someone as good-looking as Nick had scores of women, one in every town. Except for the time-sensitive project and the secret she kept, Sam wouldn't have minded being one of them.

Six

Clients staying at a CANN Isles property were ferried from a port or marina in each city to the island by private yachts either purchased or leased by the company. Less than an hour after arriving in New York City, Nick and Sam had been driven by limo to the marina in Brooklyn where the boat was docked and waiting.

"Impressive," Sam said, as the two settled at the end of circular seating that could double as a sunbathing pad on the right type of day. "CANN International most definitely does everything first class."

"Nothing you're not used to, right? The life of a princess had to have been at least this upscale. Given Nigeria is Africa's richest nation, even more so, I'd imagine."

"It was very opulent living," Sam admitted, looking out over the water.

She offered nothing more, but Nick pressed the issue. The more he interacted with Sam, the more he realized how little he knew about her. Being hesitant about getting into her personal life was understandable, but Nick was determined to get past the superficial or work conversations they had mostly had to this point.

He sat against the couch, stretched his arms across its back. "I've been to several countries in Africa, but never Nigeria. We hear so many stories. How was it living there?"

"Not like most residents, I'd suppose. Most of my life happened on the grounds of the palace, which were massive. Almost everything one could imagine for living was on the premises—pools, tennis courts, parks and spas. If something wasn't readily available, it was obtained by the staff. If it was something that I or other household members needed to personally approve, wardrobe, furniture, stuff like that, it was either handled online or personally brought in."

"That sounds super restrictive. Was it because of security concerns?"

Sam didn't answer immediately. Nick wondered if he'd overstepped.

"My ex-husband's family were very protective of not only family members but also their brand." Again, she paused, as if choosing her words carefully. "They went to great lengths to protect their privacy. However, I don't believe their actions or attention to safety went beyond that of other royals. As I said, their land holdings are massive, about an hour from Lagos, a sprawling complex that's completely secure. Life was somewhat scripted but not as rigid as it sounds."

"You loved a good party back in the day. I know you were a married woman with a child but there were no fun times on the beach or wild nights at the club?"

Sam sighed, frowned slightly. "The homes of the

wealthy are gated playgrounds. There wasn't really a need to go other places."

Nick quickly and keenly felt her mental retreat. He changed course. "Did you visit other countries?"

"Several."

"Do you have a favorite?"

"Each had its own beauty. I could live on the island of Madagascar."

"Madagascar's a sweet spot for sure. What about Maasai Mara?"

Sam shook her head. "Never heard of it. What's there?"

"Lions, cheetahs, zebras."

"A safari?"

"The best country to go on one, or so we were told. I have to admit they were right, based on the experience I had."

"What about the country where the CANN hotel is built?"

"Djibouti? Beautiful."

"How'd your brother find it?"

"You know what? Good question. You need to ask him the next time we meet."

Both slipped into silence as the boat skimmed the dark blue waters, taking them farther from the city into the deep part of the sea. Sam excused herself to call Danni and check in on Trey. Nick used the time to call the office, read his emails and return a call to his mom. Thirty minutes later, he stood and stretched as land came into view.

He walked over, opened the cabin door and yelled below. "Sam!"

"Yes?"

"We're here."

"Okay. Coming right up."

The boat docked. Within minutes, Nick and Sam were in an ATV, their luggage behind them, traveling over the bumpy terrain at a high rate of speed.

"Slow down!" Sam yelled.

Nick laughed. "Hang on. I've got this!"

As the vehicle rounded a curve and the house came into view, Sam's jaw dropped. An architectural masterpiece of glass-fiber-reinforced concrete, gleaming steel and paneless windows was far and away the most beautiful home she'd ever seen.

"This place is amazing." She spoke in a hushed, awe-inspired tone, just barely above a whisper.

"That's exactly the type of reaction we want from our guests."

Adam leaped out of the ATV, then went on the other side to let Sam out. A house employee appeared as if by magic to handle their luggage and fulfill any requests from the boss.

"The inside isn't as finished as the outside," Nick warned. "But don't let that scare you as it did the designer before you."

"Thanks for the warning," Sam replied, her heartbeat slightly quickening as they walked through an atrium filled with lush tropical plants, angel statues and an impressive waterfall. "For the inside to come anywhere close to this home's exterior is a very tall order."

Adam reached the door, then stepped back for Sam to enter. "I believe in you."

Sam stopped just inside the door. "Oh. My. Goodness." She turned to Nick. "When you said the interiors needed designing, I didn't think that meant from the studs up."

"This is one of the least finished models. Others aren't quite this bad."

"This job is way bigger than I imagined. Large crews

will be needed if there's any hope of finishing these homes in eight to twelve weeks. Have workers been lined up and contracted?"

Nick shook his head.

"No carpenters, painters, installers, nothing?"

"Again, some of the other homes are a bit further along than this but basically, many of the jobs are from the ground up."

Nick watched as Sam reached into her tote, pulled out a tablet and began jotting down notes as she walked room to room.

"I'd be lying to not admit that this feels overwhelming. Where was my luggage taken? It contains some of what I'll need to get this ball rolling. I need to get started right away."

Nick made quick work of finishing the tour, ending on the third floor of the massive mix of contemporary and bungalow styles.

"Here are the two remaining master suites," Nick pointed out, having shown her five in all. I had the maids prepare these two for our stay."

"You're staying?"

Nick worked to hide a smile. That Sam seemed concerned about the close proximity of their bedrooms pleased him more than he could let on. "Don't sound so alarmed. It's just for the night. I have an appointment in New York tomorrow morning."

"Oh, okay."

"I've got work to catch up on while you do your thing, but what say we take a break around seven for dinner tonight?"

"Thanks, but that's not really necessary. I'd rather grab something quick and continue working."

"No problem. A panel similar to the one I showed

you just beyond the foyer is also in your room and can be used to summon the chef or any of the other employees to help you. If there is anything at all that you need done, don't hesitate to ask."

"Okay, thanks, Nick. I'll see you later."

Nick retired to his room but with Sam consuming his thoughts, there was no work getting done. After basically doodling and checking social media accounts for over an hour, he donned a pair of swim trunks to douse his heated bod in the Atlantic's cold waves. Knowing Sam was down the hall would make it a challenge, but he purposely wore himself out swimming in hopes of a good night's sleep. Back at the house, he took a hot shower. Noah called just as he finished drying off. Having passed Sam downstairs hard at work on her tablet, he strode naked from his suite to the hall linen closet, looking for a particular robe he was told had been placed there, a simple terry number to replace the heavier one left in the room.

"Are you flying up or no?" he asked his twin, entering the walk-in hall closet and bypassing several robe choices before finding the one he preferred and slinging it over his shoulder. "Cool. Then let's meet at the restaurant in the office tower lobby and go over the plans before sitting down with their group."

Nick stepped out of the closet just as Sam rounded the corner.

"Oh!" she yelped, her eyes appearing to take him in like a tall glass of water in an arid desert before remembering to be professional.

"Sorry." Nick kept his eyes squarely focused on Sam as he casually slipped on the robe. "Your room is on the other side."

Sam said nothing, just wheeled around and headed in the opposite direction.

"Call you back, twin." Nick hurriedly ended the call. "Sam!"

The only response he heard was the sound of her door closing, and the lock being firmly latched behind her.

Seven

Shit! Sam reached her room, closed the door and repeated the expletive. About a dozen times. Why hadn't she paid more attention to her surroundings before leaving the room? She'd commented on the matching masters and what a good selling point that would be for potential renters. Why hadn't she focused on where she was going? And why the hello fantasy island did he have to be naked when she entered? At the thought, his image sprang into her mind. Hot. Hard. The appendage that had brought her both instant and lasting pleasure still amazingly impressive, even in its languid state. Only now did Sam think about how long it had been since she'd had sex. Too long to be on an island alone with a gorgeous man. *Shit!*

Sam jumped as her phone pinged. She picked it up. Nick.

Sorry that happened. U ok?

In her mind, sarcastic responses stumbled over each other. But her response was short and sweet.

I'm ok. ☺.

Liar. What happened wasn't okay at all. So much so that a short time later she sent Nick a second text feigning exhaustion and asked if they could meet first thing the next day. Cross-country trips and changing time zones could be tiresome, but fighting the attraction to Nick is what zapped Sam's energy. After making contact with a few of her old suppliers and surfing CANN International's website to study hotel room pics, she took a shower and slid between designer Egyptian cotton sheets. The material felt soft and seductive against her skin. The memory-foam mattress caressed her body. The pillows smelled faintly of lavender, a scent known to relax the body and quiet the mind. The combination worked wonders. Soon, Sam was fast asleep.

It seemed only moments later when the door to her room opened. Sam looked up. Nick, once again in all of his practically naked glory. He seemed ethereal, almost otherworldly, his partially clad body backlit by subdued hallway lighting. His steps were slow, measured, as he boldly approached her. He reached the foot of her bed and silently waited for an invitation to join her. Sam sat up, letting the sheet fall to reveal her bareness. Her exposed nipples pebbled quickly. Goose bumps broke out all over her ebony skin, and not just from the cool breeze through the open balcony doors. He shook the robe he wore from his shoulders, let it puddle at his feet, then crawled onto the bed like a panther, stalking its prey.

He stared deep into her eyes. Not a word had been spoken.

Sam watched as though mesmerized as Nick pulled down the sheet and exposed every inch of her body. He took a finger and slid it lazily from the heel of her foot to the insides of her thighs, flicking it along the folds of her paradise before branding her with his touch on the way back down, then sexily licking his finger. Without warning, he bent over and sucked a toe in his mouth. So delicious was his touch, so amazing, so forceful, that Sam almost had an orgasm right there!

But she didn't.

Instead, she lay back against the fluffy pillows, writhing as Nick's tongue bath continued over her ankles and shin. He kissed a sensitive spot behind her knee before trailing kisses up the insides of her thighs, gently parting her legs wider until she was fully exposed. Only seconds passed before she felt his lips touch her nether ones, before his tongue swiped the dew from between her folds, until he feasted on her feminine flower. Sam felt short of breath and tried to get away lest she die from pleasure. But Nick wasn't having it. He held her firmly by her thighs—licking, sucking, biting, kissing—until an orgasm that began at the core of her being burst forth on the waves of a scream that reverberated around the room. She lay back spent, finished.

Nick was just getting started.

He positioned himself just beyond her shoulders, his thick, stiff manhood dangling precariously close to her face. Obviously, he figured that turnabout was fair play. Who was Sam to argue? She wrapped her hands around his massive sex weapon, kissed the tip and then sucked him into her mouth. His gasp of breath let her know that she was onto something. She continued the assault, breathing him in, pulling him out, setting up a rhythm to match the pace of his hips as she ran a hand over his hard cheeks and outlined his mushroom tip with her tongue. One last thrust to her face and apparently Nick couldn't take it any longer. He pulled her up, turned her over and in one long, glorious plunge, entered her from behind.

Ah!

Sam relaxed to take in all of him before rocking back and forth in their dance of love. She moaned when he massaged her breasts and twiddled her nipples, never missing a beat as he drove himself deeper and deeper inside her, until he touched the very core. She came once, twice, but still Nick wasn't finished. He climbed off the bed, took her into his arms and walked through the open balcony doors. There, under the light of a full springtime moon, he sat on one of the lounge chairs that dotted the large balcony and directed her to sit on his still-engorged shaft. She felt like a sex goddess, watching his eyes flutter closed, feeling the wind on her sensitive buds, throwing back her hair and enjoying the ride. She rose up until only his tip was inside her, then slid down his pole like a trained firewoman. Back and forth. In and out. They made love for minutes. Or was it for hours? Or days? Finally, she felt Nick's pace quicken, heard him mumble unintelligibly until he, too, let himself go and went over the edge. The orgasm was so climactic it made her ears buzz. The sound began as if in the distance, then got louder and louder until…

She woke up.

Sam looked around the room, disoriented to find herself back in bed and not on the lounge outside. The bedsheets had been tousled and were now wrapped around her. Nick wasn't in her room. Unfortunately, she was very alone.

That had been a dream?

The buzzing she'd heard earlier sounded again. She

looked to see a light coming from the phone on the table beside her. Taking a deep breath, she picked up the receiver.

"Hello?"

"Good morning, beautiful."

"Hey, Nick."

Sam fell back against the headboard. On one hand she was glad that their making love had not happened in real time. On the other, she was sorely disappointed.

"Meeting in Manhattan got changed from lunch to breakfast but I wanted to touch base with you before leaving the island."

"You're leaving right now?"

"In about five or ten minutes. In addition to the meeting change there's a storm coming in. The captain suggested we get an early start. It sounds like I may have awakened you, though, so go ahead and finish your sleep. I imagine you have a long day ahead. We can catch up next week, when you're back home."

"Sure. I'll plan and sketch today and will forward the 3-D renderings. Perhaps we can chat by phone before I schedule contractors from the names you sent over. Thanks for those."

"No worries at all. I look forward to the sketches."

Sam heard a beep.

"Ah, I have to take this. Call me if you need me."

"Will do."

"Bye, Sam."

Just as she was about to put down her phone, a text came in. She tapped the screen. Oba. Well, wasn't that just the wake-up she needed. It was a warning to not get caught up in the feelings of her exotic dream. Because in her waking world, unless she was very careful, life could turn into a nightmare—snap—just like that.

Eight

For the next couple weeks, Nick and Sam didn't see each other but were in almost constant communication. In the mornings he'd receive detailed 3-D images of each room's design plan, sometimes updates from plans sent before. Nick appreciated that unlike the previous designer, Sam kept him apprised of the progress without being prompted. He wasn't usually a micromanager, but with the challenging timeline and the millions of dollars at stake, rest came easier knowing of any potential challenges with contractors or material deliveries and having an overview of what was happening overall. At night they'd communicate by phone, text or email, and not always about work. Nick encouraged Sam to get off the island and take advantage of being in the city that never sleeps. Sam teased at Nick that she'd do that as soon as a certain taskmaster stopped cracking the whip. While working in New York, Sam was also viewing the floor plans of the homes off the coast of Georgia and the Carolinas, which were next on the schedule. Every idea was well-thought-out and top-notch, homes to fulfill every whim of the wealthy, just as he'd envisioned.

On the professional front, all seemed to run smoothly. Yet his thought often returned to the day after he arrived in New York, and the conversation he'd had with Sam just before leaving. Nick wondered if it was his imagination, or had he heard a bit of trepidation in Sam's voice? Had she tossed and turned half the night, had trouble sleeping as had been the case with him? There was a lot on his corporate plate but Nick didn't try to fool himself. Sam being just down the hall was the reason he'd found it hard to rest that night. That more than anything is why he'd left early. The stress of another night in the same house but different beds with that woman would have taken years off his life.

Nick clicked on the 3-D image that showcased Sam's plans from an aerial perspective. He projected it from the computer to the eighty-inch wall-mounted screen, then walked over to take a more in-depth look.

A soft tap sounded behind him. Nick turned around. It was Noah. "Got a minute?"

"For you, I do. Come over and take a look at this."

Noah stopped a few feet away to fully examine the lifelike rendering, before stepping up for a closer look. He pointed to an area near the screen's left side. "Is all of this part of the atrium?"

Nick nodded. "It's already finished. And absolutely gorgeous, bro. It definitely makes an immediate statement to our guests. Sam suggested putting at least a modified version on as many homes as possible. What do you think about that?"

"What does the team think?"

"I'll find out in the meeting on Friday. Didn't you get the memo?"

"Probably. I've been tied up with Bionics all week. I'm sure Essie placed it on my calendar."

Noah's attention returned to the screen. "Do you have real photos of that?"

"I sure do. Hang on." Nick walked to his desk and reached for the mouse. His cell phone rang. A frown accompanied his greeting. "Breedlove."

"Hello?" A few seconds and then, "Who is this?" Nick sighed as he ended the call and slid the phone back to the desk.

"What was that about?" Noah asked.

"I don't know. It's been happening for a couple days now."

"Someone probably has the wrong number and keeps calling hoping that whoever they're trying to reach will answer the phone."

"You're probably right." He clicked a remote to begin the slide presentation. "Check this out."

Nick showed Noah the New York renderings and what he had so far on the other homes.

"What about Hawaii and the Bahamas?"

"Navigating the world of contractors in both locations is a bit tricky. If necessary, I'm hoping to be able to fly in the manpower we need while employing as many of the townsfolk as possible. Doing that often makes it easier for the officials to be more agreeable in other areas."

"If Sam can duplicate what's happened in New York everywhere else, she'll indeed be a miracle worker. But I don't know, man. We're into April, about ten weeks away from the first reservations. It's going to be tight."

"It's going to be amazing."

Anita interrupted via intercom. "Gentlemen, your mom is on line two."

"Who does she want to speak to?" Noah asked.

Nick picked up the phone. "Who did she call?" He pushed the blinking extension and placed the call on speakerphone. "Hey, Mom."

"Hi, Mother." Noah gave a wave as he turned and walked out the door.

"Is that Noah?"

"It was. He just left."

"Oh, dear. I hope I didn't interrupt anything."

"Just discussing trying to finish a project valued in the hundreds of millions is all."

"Oh, good. Then of course you've got time to talk with me about next month's carnival."

Nick suppressed a groan as he sat and swirled his executive chair. He knew where this conversation was heading. "All the time in the world, Mother. What's up?"

"We're finalizing the carnival's special guest list. Have you spoken with Samantha about bringing her son?"

"First of all, why are you talking about her as though she's someone you know? No one calls her Samantha, Mom. She goes by Sam."

"Duly noted. Have you asked her?"

"Honestly all I've talked about with her are the island homes."

"How are those coming along, son?"

"I'm happy to report that so far, so good. I just showed Noah the slides from what was just completed in New York, and the 3-D pictures of the next focus, which are our islands in the Southeast. Her plans look amazing."

"So did the other designer's, as I recall."

"The difference is that Sam has the reputation and

with what we've seen in New York, the experience to back up that vision."

"Sounds like this Sam is quite a woman."

"Quite the interior designer," Nick gently corrected. "That's the part of her that plays a part in my life."

Victoria chided right back. "Oh, come now, Nick. Those working alongside us have never been mere employees. Every time someone joins the corporation, our family expands."

Nick's lips went into a straight line. His grandma Jewel taught him that when one didn't have something good to say, they need say nothing at all.

"Is it possible to get Sam's email address so that I can send her a proper invitation?"

"She's really busy, Mom. I don't think—"

"Good. You don't have to. Just send over the address so that our amazing interior designer can decide for herself whether she'd want her child to attend the carnival of any child's dream."

"Send over the invitation to my cell phone, Mom. I'll forward it."

"Excellent! As soon as possible, sweetie. Have a beautiful rest of day, now. Bye-bye!"

Classic Victoria. Light a bomb, then scatter before the flame reaches the end of the wick. Being around Sam in a playful atmosphere was probably not the wisest move, but he'd do as requested and forward the invite to her. To further balk or outright refuse would only serve to make his mom that much more curious and determined. Given the pace she'd kept up for almost two weeks, Sam would probably want to spend the weekend doing something much more productive than petting animals or watching her kid's face get painted. Like sleeping.

I wouldn't mind spending the weekend sleeping in, too...with her.

The thought popped into his head before he could stop it. He was mostly successful at keeping it at bay, especially since Sam had made it clear that she didn't want to mix business with pleasure. Now with his mom's interest pricked, he definitely wanted to keep things platonic. If Victoria connected with Sam, felt she was a possible Breedlove bride and got the slightest whiff of romance, she'd start searching for suitable wedding venues and order the cake.

His phone dinged. The invite from Victoria. He clicked on it and downloaded the attachment but finished viewing Sam's latest renderings and making notes before placing the call. By then he'd mentally placed her back in the work safe zone and convinced himself that he was making too big a deal of the carnival invite. She and Trey would be two of over a thousand people his mother expected to descend on the estate next weekend.

Noah texted the invite to Sam, then got up to take in the all-encompassing Las Vegas view from his high-rise corner office. "Sam, good morning."

"Almost afternoon on the East Coast. You're calling about the Southeast island designs?"

"Yes, and something else. I just texted you an invite."

"An invite? For what?"

"Did you get it?"

"Hold on." Nick watched a plane descend toward the nearby airport. "A CANN Kind of Carnival?"

"Yes, that's it, forwarded at the specific request of my mother."

"Please join us for..." Sam's voice diminished as he imagined her quickly scanning the invitation.

"Um, yeah, this is very kind of Victoria, but I'm going to have to decline."

"About that feeling like you have an option? You don't. It's why I called."

"Let me make sure I've got this straight. My first weekend off and I'm required to attend a carnival?"

"One hosted by the CANN Foundation, which my mother heads up? Yes. It's going to be an amazing event with the proceeds benefiting children in hospitals, foster care and at-risk situations. My mom has dreamed up a ton of creative efforts over the years, but this literal fair on the grounds of the estate is a first."

"And you're saying this is mandatory?"

"I'm saying it would be in your best interest."

"Why? I don't remember attending CANN charity events being in my agreement."

"Mom knows you're new to town and a single mother. She feels an outing like this would be a great way for you and Trey to meet other moms and young kids in the community."

"That's very thoughtful of her, but honestly, I was looking forward to a simple weekend, a movies-and-pizza kind of affair. Especially with the Carolinas on the schedule next week and a few potential material availability fires already cropping up. Since you're such an ace business negotiator, why don't you decline the RSVP on my behalf."

"Because Victoria is a partner possessing debate skills that make winning arguments darn near impossible. I believe the invitation allows you to include a friend or two. Perhaps your cousin or another mother would like to join you? As much as I appreciate your focus, a short break from the stress might do you good. You'll enjoy yourself and your son will love it."

After a pause, Sam responded. "I'm sure he'd have fun. I could probably find an hour or two to hang out there."

"Good."

She chuckled. "Is that relief I hear in your voice?"

"Ha! Picked up on that, did you? If you knew Mom, you'd be relieved, too."

"I don't understand."

"Victoria Breedlove lives life on a chessboard. She never makes one move without having thought three or four moves ahead. I've played on this board all my life and know for sure that it would be better to say yes to this invitation and have whatever conversation she obviously wants to have with you, than to decline and make her even more determined to make a connection."

"Does she know about us, I mean, our one-night stand?"

"No."

"Does she usually meet with or invite all new employees to charitable functions?"

"I can't say that she does. Look, I don't want to frighten you. But you might as well know that you'll be under the V-radar. Mom looked you up online. She saw your picture, thinks you're gorgeous, is familiar with your work and is an incurable matchmaker. She'll more than likely want to get all up in your business and has the uncanny knack to be halfway through your personal secrets chest before you realize the lid has been opened. Be cordial, but know that you are under no obligation whatsoever to share anything outside of casual pleasantries. I'll introduce you to the girls, who between the three of them can share a bevy of appropriate diversionary comebacks."

"The girls...your in-laws."

"My in-loves—Lauren, Ryan and Dee."

"Ah, right."

Nick heard the sound of a beep and a whispered expletive on the other end of the line.

"Nick, I've got to go."

"Everything all right?"

"It will be."

The line went dead.

In the world of construction, delays, snags, errors and snafus came with the territory. The angst heard in Sam's voice was not uncommon, especially given the scope and scale of what they were building. Yet it bothered him to hear it, to think that something was dimming the light in those gorgeous brown eyes.

A few minutes later, his cell phone rang. Unknown caller. Again.

"Breedlove." A slight rustling was heard on the otherwise silent line. "Hello? Who is this? Look, whoever you're looking for is not at this number. Do not call it again."

Nick ended the call more than a bit chagrined. The calls were increasing to the point of becoming a nuisance. An unknown number could not be blocked. Much like the errant erotic thoughts that kept springing up about Sam.

He couldn't block them. That bothered him, too.

Nine

Every part of Sam's mind was exhausted. With the unexpected delays and back-ordered materials, her stay on the idyllic island was by no means a vacation. But she'd gotten the job done. Except for the furnishings that had been ordered but not yet delivered, CANN Isle-New York was finished, enough so that Sam felt confident moving on to the Carolinas next week. After speaking with Danni about the woman she'd hired to look after Trey, and watching the nanny's interaction with her son, she also felt very good about hiring Gloria Monroe.

"Come on, little man. I've got him, Gloria, thanks."

Sam reached into the car seat and pulled the sleeping tyke from the car seat, then followed an equally tired live-in nanny into the condo. The driver pulled their luggage from the trunk and deposited it at the entrance.

"Would you like me to take these inside, ma'am?"

"No, that's okay. We can get it from here." She reached inside her purse and pulled out a bill. "Thank you."

"I appreciate it, ma'am. Have a good night."

While Gloria handled the luggage, Sam continued on to Trey's room. She set down her purse and undressed her son. She'd just pushed his last extremity into his favorite Black Panther superhero pajamas when her phone rang.

She fished it out of her bag, placed it on Trey's bed and pushed the speaker button. "Hey, cuz, can I call you right back? I just got home and am putting Trey to bed."

"Okay. Call ASAP."

Sam's brow creased. Danielle didn't sound happy. Sam tucked Trey into bed, proceeded to her room and even though she wanted nothing more than a quick hot shower and her soft, warm bed, she had a brief chat with Gloria, giving her the weekend off, then retreated to the master.

She hit Redial. "I've got a date with a pillow, cousin, so make it quick. What's up?"

"I'm not sure you want to know, but you need to."

The cryptic answer pushed a bit of Sam's exhaustion away. She sat straighter on the bed. "You don't sound good, Danni. What's going on?"

Sam heard a deep sigh on the other end of the line.

"I recently met up with a few girlfriends. One of them had heard talk." A beat and then, "About you."

"Me? I barely even live here. Who can say what about me?"

"Not as much you as Trey."

Sam's blood cooled. When she spoke her tone was low, deadly. "What is being said about my son?"

"The word is out that Oba is not Trey's biological dad, and a few nosy Nancys are speculating on the father."

"Why don't they speculate on minding their business?"

"You working with one of the town's most eligible

bachelors makes you their business. Especially Joi, who's obviously been running her big mouth."

"Dammit."

"I know, girl. I almost called you the night I found out but I know how busy this job has got you—figured tonight would be soon enough."

"You know what? I'm not totally surprised. Oba's been calling."

"No way. For how long?"

"Off and on since I've been here. But they really ramped up a few weeks ago when his dad kicked him out of the palace. Said he needed help maintaining his lifestyle."

"And he thought you, a single, working mother, was the one to give it to him?"

"When I told him I didn't have any money, he suggested I ask Nick. There was a barely veiled threat with the request but honestly I thought he was bluffing. Now, with what you're telling me, and especially at the mention of his sister, the recent conversations make even more sense."

"There always was something about that girl. Don't get me wrong, she has a kind side. We've always been cool and used to hang out all the time before the kids came along. It's how she gossiped and talked about others that used to bug me, and the way she treated those she considered subpar. I guess because her messiness was never directed toward me, I ignored it. I shouldn't have. Asking Nick for the money may have even been her idea."

"Probably. She's how he found out we were working together."

"And the only other person who knew that Oba wasn't Trey's father."

"Until Isaac sneaked a piece of Trey's hair, had a DNA test done and ensured their whole family knew the truth."

"I think it was Joi. Like I said, she's got a messy side."

Sam flopped back on her bed. "I've got to tell Nick, now, at the worst possible time."

"While the two of you are working so closely together."

"That's not all." Sam told Danielle about the carnival happening that weekend. "I can invite a guest. Will you go? Please?"

"Absolutely, I'll go. Jaylen and Trey will have a ball. You'll be fine, too. It may feel like the end of the world, Sam. But it's not."

The next morning, Sam slept in and enjoyed a light breakfast with just her and Trey before getting them dressed for their outing.

Once in the car, Trey asked, "Where are we going, Mama?"

"First, to pick up Danni and Jaylen and then to a town called Breedlove."

"What's in Bead Love?"

"It's BREED-love, honey, and it's a surprise."

Less than forty-five minutes later, Sam bypassed the stately wrought iron privacy gates to the Breedlove Estate and continued via the texted instructions to a tree-lined side road about a half a mile down from the family mansion. Signs had been erected welcoming guests to the CANN CARNIVAL, with directions to parking lots and the main entrance. Rounding the corner, Sam couldn't believe her eyes. A fairground rivaling any town, big or small, had been erected on Breedlove land. The boys squealed, their heads pressed to the glass as they chatted excitedly.

"A carnival!"

"With rides and everything!"

Upon reaching the entrance and receiving a map to the grounds and armbands allowing free rides and other niceties for special guests, Sam sent Nick a text.

I'm here, FYI. Wow. Amazing!

The women had their hands full with two wide-eyed boys and put them on the first available ride simply to catch their breath.

The ride finished. Nick texted back. Where are you?

Near entrance. Boys on the first ride they saw.

☺ There will be a raffle in the casino in an hour. Meet me there.

Sam referenced the map as the group made their way around the carefully planned scene. There was a Ferris wheel, merry-go-rounds, carnival games and a petting zoo. There were bumper cars and a video arcade, along with more adventuresome rides for teens. The adults hadn't been left out, either. Towering zip lines and soaring rock-climbing walls had been erected aside more traditional rides like the Kamikaze and Tilt-A-Whirl. A large tent housed the mini-CANN casino described on the back of the map, complete with slot machines and poker, blackjack and roulette tables. Music and other sounds filled the air. Dotted throughout were food trucks and sweets stands. In short, Nick's mom had organized a child's best dream. The meticulously manicured lawns had been carefully turned into a Memorial Day wonderland for both the young and the young at heart.

An hour later and Sam still wasn't ready to face Nick.

She was sure that meant meeting his mom and possibly other members of his family.

"Why don't I take the boys to the petting zoo?" Danielle offered.

Sam could have kissed her. "That's a perfect idea. Keep your phone handy. I'll text you when I'm done."

She watched her cousin and the boys walk away, then crossed over to and stepped inside the casino. After pausing for her eyes to adjust to the dimmed lighting, she looked around and spotted Nick almost immediately. He looked up to catch her staring, smiled and waved her over. Sam gave herself a pep talk, remembering Danielle's parting words before she left with the boys. *They don't know anything until you tell them. Remember that.*

"Hey, Nick."

"There she is. The miracle worker!" Nick pulled Sam into an enthusiastic hug. "Congrats on a bang-up job out there. Our New York guests are in for a treat."

Sam was embarrassed at the show of affection but appreciative of the praise. She was also über-aware of other eyes on her. "One down, twenty-plus to go. Let's not pop the cork yet."

"Just a matter of time," Nick responded, full of confidence. "I picked the one person in the world who could get the job done."

At this, an older woman standing near him, who even in casual slacks and an oversize top oozed refinement and class, smiled and held out her hand.

"You must be Samantha. I'm Victoria, Nick's mom."

"It's a pleasure to meet you, Victoria. Please, call me Sam. Thank you so much for the special invitation to attend this spectacular event. My son is already over the moon. He won't want to leave."

Victoria looked to both sides of Sam. "Where is your son?"

"With his cousin visiting the petting zoo."

"Always a child favorite. I'm glad he's having a good time."

A young woman walked up. "Excuse me, Victoria, but it's time for the raffle."

"Of course. We'll talk more later, Sam, all right?"

No, it was not all right. "Sure."

During the raffle, Sam met Noah, Adam and Christian. Their wives and several others assisted Victoria on stage. The guys were fun and easygoing. Sam was happy to know she'd overreacted. What could go wrong at a carnival, where folk walked around with big smiles on their faces? Even after the raffle, when Nick insisted on walking with her to meet back up with Danielle, Sam only felt the slightest of flutters. Nick didn't yet know what she hadn't told him. There's no way he'd have an inkling that Trey was his. Nick had a light complexion. Trey had inherited his mom's richly melanated skin. Trey was tall for his age but he was still only four, bearing hardly a hint of resemblance to the six-feet-plus of deliciousness his father carried around.

"Danni, you remember Nick?" she said, once she and Danielle reunited.

Danielle smiled. "Of course. Nice to see you again."

"Likewise." Nick shook her hand.

"Trey, Jaylen, this is Nick. I work with him building houses."

Nick knelt to their level and held out his hand. "Hello, Trey. Hello, Jaylen. Are you boys having a good time?"

"Yes!" They sang in duet.

"Uncle Nick!" A high-pitched yell rose over the din

of noises before a little girl wearing pink overalls and a straw hat burst through the crowd.

As soon as she reached him, he scooped her up. "Hey, Angel!"

"My name's not Angel, it's Christina!"

"But you look like an angel."

Curls bounced as the four-year old shook her head from side to side. "I don't look like an angel. I don't have wings!"

Christian strolled up to them. "Another debate within seconds? You two never see the world the same."

"Which is what makes life so exciting," Nick said, easing Christina to the ground. "The world opens up wider when viewed through the eyes of a child."

Christian turned to Sam. "Do you believe that?"

"Sometimes."

Nick put an arm around Sam. "Good answer. Where's Lar?"

Nick looked around for Christina's little brother, Larenz, and saw Christian's wife Lauren pushing a stroller. Sam quietly watched the family's interactions. The adults, thoroughly enjoying each other, the kids clearly loved. This was the life her secret kept from Trey. It wasn't fair and considering the rumblings, it wasn't wise, either.

"You know what, Nick. I need to speak with you about something."

"Okay."

"Uncle Nick!" Christina interrupted. "Can you take me to ride the horses?"

"We can ride them?" Trey asked wide-eyed.

Danielle looked toward the large white tent where she'd taken the boys. "I didn't see horses at the petting zoo."

"They're not a part of the carnival. They're on Adam's ranch."

"Horses," Trey cried. "I want to ride horses!"

Sam took the arm of a child on his way out of control. "Trey! Come on, honey. The horses aren't here. Let's go ride the merry-go-round or Ferris wheel."

"Those horses are fake," he announced, spitting out the last word as if it were vile, before doing something he rarely did. Began to throw a fit. "Horses! I want to ride the horses!" Screaming and crying, with Sam looking at him as she would a stranger.

Whose child is this?

"Hey, hey, hey." Nick knelt until they were face-to-face. "Trey, look at me. Only big boys can ride the horses. With you crying like that, and screaming and stomping, you'll scare them away. Trey, do you hear me?"

Somewhere in his wall of hollers Nick's words sank through. The crying stopped as quickly as it started.

"Yes," he answered, throwing in a sniffle for good measure.

Sam watched, amazed and more than a little touched. Their first father-son interaction and neither of them knew it.

"Mom, can I go ride the horses? I'm not crying now."

Sam looked at Nick, who only now realized his error.

"You said it."

"I did, didn't I." He lifted Trey into the crook of his arm. "Tell you what. The horse I have in mind for you to ride doesn't like crowds. But if you act like the little man that I believe you can be for the rest of the day, I'll ask Mommy to bring you back in the morning, and we'll go riding then. But you have to be good. Your mom will tell me if you're not. Deal?"

Trey nodded in reluctant agreement.

"Is that okay with you?" Nick asked Sam.

"Well, since you've just made a huge promise to a four-year-old," she said under her voice before announcing, "I guess…yes."

"Sorry." Nick talked softly as well so that only Sam could hear. "I guess I shouldn't have done that. In my effort to come off as the savior, I've committed you to another day at the fair, or back here to ride horses at least."

"Worse could happen."

"Indeed."

The group split up soon after the convo ended. Sam and Danielle ended up staying much longer than they'd planned and enjoyed the goings-on possibly more than adults should. For Sam, it was the first time since accepting the contract that she allowed herself to unwind, to forget about materials and drawings and deadlines and simply have a good time. By the time moms and sons left the fairgrounds, both Sam and Danielle were glad they'd brought strollers. The kids were knocked out.

"How did it feel to see—" Danielle tilted her head toward the back seat "—with his father."

"It's hard to describe." Sam caught a mental image of Nick picking up Trey. "I didn't know there was that much love in my heart."

"For the son…or the daddy?"

"I can't help but love Nick. He's the father of my child. But that and my temporary boss is all that he is."

Danielle let it go and changed the subject. Sam was glad that she did. The truth of the matter was that she wanted Trey to get to know Nick better and looked forward to tomorrow. Hopefully the more Nick felt an affinity with Trey, the easier it would be to accept that he was his son, too.

That night she lay in bed thinking. *It's coming to-*

gether. I may be able to rebuild my life after all. The good feeling lasted a full fifteen minutes, until her phone buzzed and she read the text that had just come in from overseas. Without checking the name, she knew who it was.

No more asking. No more waiting. Wire 500K to my bank account before the end of the month. Or I tell Nick everything.

Ten

Nick took a seat at the long patio table on his parents' back porch, then waved away his twin, who'd prepared to sit beside him.

Noah's brow raised. "Are we expecting someone?"

"I invited Sam over. Yesterday Christina mentioned riding horses in front of her son and suddenly the Merry-Go-Round became a poor second choice."

Noah walked around to sit across from Nick. "So Sam's bringing him over to go riding?"

"Yep. You're welcome to join us."

"Thanks, bro, but I'm going to stay close to sweet lady. She's had a couple premature contractions and chose to stay home."

"Makes sense. Then why are you here?"

"To pick up the cinnamon rolls she craves. And now that I know Sam is joining us…to stick around a little while for the show."

Nick knew Noah was talking about the creative ways their mother tended to question any female she deemed clan-suitable. While his mother had only spoken casually with Sam yesterday, that she'd done online research was enough for him to know his designer was on her radar.

Brunch was in full swing when one of the housekeepers brought Sam, Trey and another woman around to the back. Nick took in her unsure expression and met her at the patio's edge to make her welcome.

"There they are! Hey guys." He noticed a dip in conversation as the duo approached.

Nick knelt down. "How are you, little man?"

"Fine."

"Ready to ride horses?"

"Yes!"

He turned to Sam. "Hello."

"Hi." She looked at the woman beside her. "I hope you don't mind that I brought my nanny, Gloria. She was so excited by what I shared yesterday that I felt bad at not inviting her."

"No worries. She can join Chris's au pair Kirtu in the other room with Christina and Lars."

He looked beyond her. "No Danni today?"

"Like me, she's never ridden a horse. Unlike me, she'd like to keep it that way." After brief instructions to Trey on how to behave, he and Gloria headed toward the kids' room.

"You've never taken a ride before?" Nick asked, leading them toward the buffet line. He noticed Sam's eyes flicker just enough to confirm she'd caught the double entendre. "No, I've never before ridden a horse, though I once caravanned on a camel."

"I thought you'd never gone on a safari?"

"I haven't. That ride occurred during a tour of the Egyptian pyramids."

"There you go! You'll be fine."

After walking through the buffet line and loading up their plates, they took their seats at the table.

"Everybody, you remember Sam from yesterday? Those who weren't there, this is Sam Price, the extraordinary interior designer who's ensuring our island guests are properly blown away by their surroundings."

A variety of greetings rang out from the dozen or so gathered around the table. Small talk ensued, mostly about the success of the CANN Carnival, raising millions of dollars for children needing assistance in Nevada and beyond.

During a lull in the conversation, Victoria spoke. "Samantha, I understand you recently moved back from being an expat in Africa. Do you miss that beautiful continent or were you happy to return home?"

"You're right, Victoria, there are areas of Africa that are absolutely stunning, some of the most beautiful scenery I've seen. But I'm very glad to be back in the States."

"Well, I can tell you that Nick for one is glad you're back as well. He sings your praises as a designer."

Sam smiled at Nick. "Thank you." Then to Victoria, "CANN is an excellent company. I am thankful to have gotten such a wonderful opportunity so soon after arriving."

"You two seem to get along very well. Did you know each other prior to coming on board for the island project?"

"Aren't these crepes delicious?" Noah asked, a question so unlike what he'd normally ask that everyone knew its purpose and laughed at the blatant subject change to bail out his twin.

Nick stuffed a bite in his mouth and talked while chewing. "Ah, bro, they're delish!"

"For sure," Adam added. "With these sweet potato crepes Gabe has outdone himself!"

The conversation was successfully diverted long enough for Nick and Sam to finish their dishes and make a graceful exit. They stopped next door where the kids were playing board games. With Gloria and a very excited Trey in tow, they headed toward Adam's ranch and the stable of horses he kept there.

Nick introduced Sam to the ranch manager, Rusty, who walked them over to where Adam's growing collection of prized horses was housed. He picked an apple from a barrel near the barn's entrance and gave it to Nick.

"For when the little one meets Queen."

"Ah, good choice," Nick said, about the gentle mare. "Little man and I will be riding together." Rusty nodded. "We'll want someone equally gentle for Sam here. It's her first time riding."

"No worries, pretty lady," Rusty said. "We'll get you fixed right up." He gave them apples, too.

Sam turned to Gloria. "Am I the only one on a maiden voyage, or have you not ridden before either?"

"It's been a long time ago, back in Oklahoma on my grandpa's farm."

"It's like riding a bike," Rusty assured her. "Sit the saddle properly and it's all downhill from there."

When they reached Queen, Nick handed Trey the apple. "One of these always helps to make a proper introduction."

Trey took the apple and was properly awed as Nick guided his hand for the horse to softly remove it, then picked him up to pet Queen's mane.

Nick winked at Sam. "He's a natural, same as Noah and I were when we were his age."

The four got saddled up—Nick and Trey on Poker, Gloria on an Appaloosa named Lucy, and Sam on Queen. Gloria's was an easy mount, but Sam needed help. Nick was happy to oblige. Any excuse to caress her glorious backside would do. Queen began to prance. Sam tensed up right away.

"Just relax," Nick said, his tone low and soothing. "Animals can smell fear. Hold the reins with confidence. She needs to know you're in control."

"That's still up for debate."

Nick helped Sam until she felt more comfortable, walking them around in a circle near the gate.

"You ready?"

Sam nodded. "I think so."

With that, they took off across the glorious countryside at a comfortable pace. Even after spending his entire life on the land, Nick was still moved by its beauty. After about ten minutes, when he felt Sam had a handle on Queen, Nick gave his horse his head and sped up a bit. Trey squealed with delight. Nick focused on Trey, even as he himself enjoyed the chance to get out in nature and feel the wind on his face. All the brothers had grown up in the saddle, but he and Christian rode far less often than Noah and Adam. Today reminded Nick he needed to change that.

"Let's go fast again, Nick!"

"Okay, buddy." Nick secured Trey in his grip, then lightly touched the horse's flank.

"Nick!"

"Don't worry, Sam! I've got him."

"It's Sam, Nick!"

Nick turned toward the sound of Gloria's voice in time

to observe Queen's trot increasing to a gallop at a quick pace. Sam must have unknowingly directed the horse to run. Without thought, he wheeled Poker around and headed toward Sam.

"Relax, Sam! Don't pull so hard on the reins!"

Nick quickly eased alongside Sam and grabbed the horse's reins. Within seconds, the horse slowed down. Nick made a few sounds and talked to Queen until the horse came to a stop.

"You all right?" He'd been so busy getting the horse under control that only now did he see the tears in Sam's eyes, or that an ashy sheen to her deep chocolate skin alluded to how frightened she was, as did the shaky hand that had grabbed him once he was close with nails now almost piercing his cotton shirt.

Nick didn't need to hear her answer. She was not okay.

By the time the horse stopped, Gloria had rounded back to where they all were. "Can you ride with Trey?" he asked her.

She nodded. "I think so."

"Good. Because Sam's going to ride with me." Nick glanced at his watch. "The carnival opens in an hour. We'd planned to go to the house to freshen up anyway. We'll just do that now."

Nick helped Sam into the saddle, then mounted behind her. Immediately, he knew he was in trouble. Sam's body, warm, curvaceous and shaking, folded into his embrace. For the woman he'd always seen as strong and confident, the vulnerability was foreign. The need to protect her sprang up with force in his chest. He felt capable and needed, feelings that opened up a space for Sam in his heart. Instinctively, a protective arm went around her. He tilted his hips back in an effort to hide an oncoming arousal, but Sam followed his body with her own, as if his touch alone reassured her. It made him powerful; his testosterone surged. He grew heady from the scent of her cologne, the feel of her soft locs brushing against his neck and chest and her body folded into his own. By the time they reached his home, he was on fire with desire, felt almost drunk with need. He helped her down, then took the horse around back and dismounted in private, until his own privates were under control.

She was standing by the window when he entered, seemingly still as shaken in his living room as she'd been outside.

Gloria stood near her, a concerned look on her face. Trey hid behind Gloria's legs. "Is there anything I can do for you?"

"I'll be okay."

Nick watched Sam attempt a reassuring smile for her observant son. He guessed she was trying to assure herself as well.

Nick's doorbell rang. He frowned slightly at the unexpected intrusion. "Who could that be?" he murmured.

"It's probably Kirtu," Gloria offered. "We talked about meeting up so that the children could continue playing together. I'll tell her we'll meet later on."

Sam shook her head. "No, please, you guys go on to the carnival and text your location. I'll be along shortly."

Nick opened the door. Indeed it was Christina's nanny. She spoke to everyone.

"Where's Christina?" Gloria asked.

"With Lauren. They're spending a bit of time together before she goes off with Christian. We're supposed to meet them at the food court."

Gloria turned to Sam once again. "Are you sure?"

"Absolutely, Gloria." Sam looked at Trey. "Are you ready for more rides and games, Trey?"

Trey reached for Gloria's hand and vigorously nodded.

"Good. I'll meet you there in a little bit. If you leave that area, Gloria, just text me where you are. All right?"

"Sure."

As soon as Trey was gone, Sam collapsed against the wall. "Crap! That was scary!"

Nick was immediately by her side. "I'm sorry, babe. I've ridden Queen many times and seen others ride her. You must have unknowingly given her the signal to run. Doing so on her own would be very uncharacteristic.

"How about some hot chamomile tea. Or something stronger if you'd like."

Sam managed a smile. "Tea is fine. Thanks again, Nick," she whispered, flinging her arms around his neck, pressing her body against him. "I don't know what I would have done without your help earlier. I'm so glad you were there."

Nick was glad he was there, too, and that Sam was in his arms. It felt good, too good. He gently gripped her arms and meant to set her away from him. But just then she turned her face so that their lips were parallel, then pressed those soft cushions of sexy goodness against his eager lips. Whatever control he had went out the window. He placed his hands beneath her butt and lifted her up against the wall, his lips never leaving hers as he secured himself between her legs.

"Nick."

Sam's voice was light, shaky, caught up in ecstasy. He watched, mesmerized, as she reached for the hem of her top and pulled it over her head. Then to the back of her bra, snapping the clasp from the back. Everything she did was everything he'd imagined. The switch had happened so quickly he felt it almost surreal, as though he were an observer instead of a participant, needing to be prodded to play along.

"Nick, please..."

Her soft entreaty was all the encouragement he needed. He pulled a soft nipple into his mouth, unzipping his jeans while he feasted. They kissed every part of exposed flesh available, and quickly realized that was not enough. They needed more, much more. They needed all of each other.

Sam slid from the wall and reached for her pants. They quickly joined Nick's in a pile on the floor. He lifted her once again and placed her on the living room's oversize ottoman. The bedroom was too far away, would take too long to consummate a reunion more than four years in the making. Dropping down in front of her, Nick gently spread her legs apart. He slid a finger along the folds of her thong and after pushing it aside, buried his head in her heat. She squealed and squirmed but he gave no quarter. He lapped and lavished her pearl, feasted on her nectar. Her soft thighs rested on his shoulders, gripping him hard as she reached and then went over the edge. Her whimpers sent his dick rock hard. He retrieved a condom from his pants pocket, positioned his shaft where his tongue had been and deepened the dance.

"Nick, Nick," she purred, in beat with this rhythm. He thrust and plunged himself into her core, grabbed the juicy cheeks that drove him wild and ground deeply some more. Their bodies came together like two long-lost pals who'd known each other forever, who'd always loved this way. They ended up in the bedroom, where Sam performed oral feats that left Nick shaken to the bone, that made him forget about every other woman who in the throes of passion had ever called his name. When he felt Sam ready to burst again, he increased his thrusts to join her going over the edge. There was one woman on his mind, one name on his lips. He whispered it as he shuddered.

"Sam."

Eleven

Sam's orgasm had barely ended before regret set in. Not that she and Nick had sex. In retrospect, the act seemed a foregone conclusion from the time she'd stepped in his office on that first interview. An ending they both saw coming but tried to ignore. No, Sam's regret was about what had been unleashed inside her. Rekindled. Reawakened. It was the feeling she'd had the first time she saw Nick. A palpable hunger. An undeniable connection. But leading to what? Even now, as Nick stood behind her, held her, kissed her neck and nibbled her ear as the shower water washed over them, Sam felt a longing in her heart for something she feared Nick could not fulfill, or wasn't interested in fulfilling.

"We need to hurry," she whispered, stepped away from him and reaching for a loofah on one of the shelves. She quickly unwrapped it, performed her ablutions and left the bathroom. By the time Nick came out she was dressed and on her phone, texting Gloria as to her and Trey's whereabouts. She went to the kitchen and reheated the tea that had earlier been poured and forgotten, added cream and sugar, then took small sips to calm her nerves. This helped her put the tiger of desire back in its cage, regain control of her body and rid her mind of happily ever after fantasies that only came true in romance novels.

He walked straight toward her. "That was amazing, babe."

She dodged his intended embrace and put distance between them. "We need to talk about what just happened."

A smile slid onto Nick's face, as slow as molasses and Sam knew, equally sweet. "I hope you're not expecting that talk to include an apology, because I am not at all sorry about being with you. In fact, I want to do it again. Soon. And often."

Sam worked to stay focused on what needed to be said and not how good Nick looked in the white tee, low-slung black jeans and sandals that now covered the body that had so pleasured her just moments ago. Hard to do. Every movement reminded her of something he'd done. How the fingers fastening his belt buckle had played her body like an instrument, had trailed from the back of her neck to her thighs and left goose bumps in their wake. How his soft, thick lips had touched, branded, almost every inch of her body, and how his tongue had—for those few intimate seconds, or hours, who's counting—wiped away every worry about Oba, Trey's parentage, the projects and everything else. She turned away as he looked up, convinced that the desire dredged up by those too-recent memories were written all over her face.

She took a breath and began again, her back toward him as she walked to an abstract painting hung on the wall. "No regrets, it's not about that. Or the attraction," she continued, boldly turning to face not only her fears, but him as well. "Which especially after what just happened, I won't try to deny. This is about you being my boss. And me having a job to do. A physical relationship might get in the way of that."

He smiled in obvious agreement.

The grip on her mug of tea tightened. "It would definitely get in the way."

"You're probably right." His eyes never left hers while raising a bottle of water to his lips.

Both sipped in silence.

"That's it?" Sam finally asked.

Nick shrugged. "What else can there be? I don't agree with your position but your message is clear."

"I don't want this to create an awkward vibe between us."

"We're both adults. I don't foresee a problem if you don't. Although I don't think tamping down what's flowing between us will be as easy as you think. I mean, damn. What happens when we're together, the way our bodies fit like perfect puzzle pieces, the way you mold around me like a custom-made glove…"

Damn if hearing that sexy voice and seeing that lethal tongue didn't make her want to do it again. "Nick, stop. I'm serious."

"So am I. Look, beautiful, may I suggest something?"

Not in the voice that makes my panties wet. "What?"

"Why don't we relax around what's happening, not make any rules or resist what is abundantly clear. I'm not dating anyone right now, are you?"

"No, but…"

"No buts. I get that you want to focus on business. I respect that and will be a total gentleman. I won't do anything you don't want to do. I'm just saying that if the situation arises, as it did just now, let's deal with it then, in the moment, and see what happens."

"Okay." Sam's phone buzzed. She checked it. "That's Gloria. She and Kirtu are with the kids in the Fun Zone."

"Do you want to get your face painted, too?" Nick teased.

"No, but I might accept one of the clown's animal balloons…since I feel like an ass," she finished, mumbling under her breath.

"What was that?"

"Nothing."

Sam was determined to try Nick's approach. She tried to act casual, as if it were just another day. But as they neared the crowded fairgrounds, she felt that the fact she'd just been screwed to within an inch of her life and loved every second of it was readily apparent. If so, however, Gloria didn't let on. She relaxed even more and instead of feeling paranoid with Nick beside her allowed herself to enjoy his company. He really was amazing with children. Clearly his niece adored him.

"Hi, Uncle Nick!"

"Come here, Angel." He easily lifted Christina into his arms.

Trey, feeling left out, whined to also be held in Nick's arms. "Pick me up! Pick me up, too!"

Sam prepared to admonish him, but Nick complied. He reached down, easily balancing a child in each arm. They laughed at the kids' obvious attempts to garner the most attention from a man both children clearly liked. So caught up was she in the joy of the moment that danger sidled up beside her undetected.

"Nick, or Noah?"

Sam turned to see a beautiful woman with flawless skin and long black hair peering carefully between the kids and Nick. The smile Nick put on Sam's face with his lovemaking and charming personality slid off faster than she'd slid off Queen earlier. The last person on earth that she wanted to see appeared like an apparition before her.

Joi.

Nick looked at her. "I'm sorry. Do I know you?"

"Not really." Joi smiled at him while looking every inch of amazing, and seductive. "We've met socially a couple times. A few years ago, we were at the same costume party, in fact."

She slid a quick glance at Sam. Sam stopped breathing.

"My name's Joi." Nodding toward the children Nick was placing back on the ground, she said with hand outstretched, "Which one is yours?"

Nick uncoiled back to his full height. "Nick."

Joi shook Nick's hand, then looked at Trey standing close by Nick's side and tried to shake his, too. Trey pulled it back. Sam stopped herself from stepping between them.

"Hello, little one! Is this your son, Nick?"

"No. Trey belongs to this beautiful lady, Sam Price."

Joi turned, eyes wide in feigned surprise. "Sam!"

Sam had the distinct feeling her presence was not a surprise to her former sister-in-law. She worked to keep a WTF look off her face.

"Oh my goodness, I was so focused on Nick and those cute little kids I didn't see you!"

"A woman you've known for years?" *And a child who's your nephew?* Sam so wanted to add that line, but now wasn't the time. "I find that hard to believe but…okay."

Joi leaned into Sam for a hug. It was like embracing a board. "Don't play me," Joi quietly hissed. "Or you'll get played."

Not a hint of meanness showed when she stepped

back, all smiles and bright, wide eyes. Joi was a beautiful girl, Sam decided, whose performance could have easily won an Oscar.

What an actress. It was incredible that the same woman who appeared as an angel years ago could behave so much like the devil right now. Her threat answered one question. Joi may not have suggested that Oba blackmail her for money, but Sam was convinced that Joi was somehow involved. Their knowing what Nick didn't was a very real threat to Sam getting back on her feet. But she'd be damned if she let Joi think they held an advantage. When pressed, Sam could be an actor, too.

"I heard the news about your getting a job with CANN International."

"I heard you've been spreading quite a bit of news about me and you need to stop." Said as quietly as Joi's warning, and as sweetly as though honey had been poured over the words. But the glint in Sam's eyes conveyed "don't start none, won't be none."

A slight narrowing of Joi's eyes was the only hint that Sam's words had hit a mark.

"You two obviously know each other," Nick said, as tension crackled.

"We're family," Joi replied, with a fake laugh that made Sam's skin crawl. Her mind whirled with possible motives for Joi being here. None of them were good.

Sam turned to Nick. "Not anymore. Joi is my ex-husband's sister. She's how he and I met."

"Ah, I see." Nick looked at Joi with renewed interest and an unreadable expression. Sam imagined that information caused him to look at this overly friendly interruption in a new light. "Yet you didn't recognize Trey?"

Good question, Sam thought. Would-be actress Joi didn't miss a beat.

"It's been a couple years since I've seen him. He was just a baby when a myriad of business opportunities brought me back to live full-time in the States. He's gotten so big!"

She looked pointedly at Sam. "Wonder where he gets his height? My brother is average height, as are most men on that side of the family."

"My brother's tall," Sam said before reaching for Trey's hand. "So is my dad. It's understandable you'd be confused since you never met my side of the family, and since the few interactions we had at the palace were too brief and infrequent to develop a bond."

"Since we're both back in America, maybe we can change that. You and Oba are divorced. But I'm still Trey's aunt, right?"

In light of no good answer, Sam remained mum.

Sam didn't want to leave Joi alone with Nick, but she couldn't stay and watch the Oscar-worthy performance one moment longer. There would come a moment when Sam could tell Joi just what she thought of this messy charade. But not today.

"We've got a date with a puppet or two," Sam finally said, forcing a casualness into her voice that she didn't feel.

"Hang on," Nick said. "I'll bring Christina."

"Enjoy the fair," Nick said, already turning to walk away from Joi.

"Goodbye, Joi!" Sam kept her voice light, tried to hide how much she'd been affected by the exchange. She was only partly successful. The smile in Sam's voice did not reach her eyes.

When they neared the tent where the puppet theater was housed, Sam sent Trey in with Gloria. Nick followed suit with Christina and her au pair. Once alone, Nick's concern was immediate.

"You okay?"

"Why wouldn't I be?" Sam snapped back. It was enough that Joi had come and effectively ruined what in spite of her roiling, disjointed emotions and unplanned romp in the sack with her boss had been a pretty awesome day. Had Nick picked up on it?

"That was a pretty tense situation back there."

Yes, he had.

Sam shrugged. "Joi's known for starting trouble. I don't care much for folk like that."

"Yet she's the one who introduced you to your ex."

"I rest my case."

Nick chuckled. "I don't remember ever meeting her. Then again, I meet a lot of people so it's entirely possible that she and I traveled in the same circles. As I always say, this town is small."

"Speaking of small, I'm going in." She nodded toward the theater tent. "Are you coming?"

"No. I think I've met my kid-stuff quota for today. I was going to suggest we become kids ourselves and enjoy some of the adult rides."

"Thanks, Nick, but I'm going to have to pass. I head to South Carolina first thing tomorrow and have quite a bit to get done. After this show, I'm going to take Trey home."

"Come here." Before Sam could react, she'd been pulled into Nick's arms. "Today was amazing," he whispered, his voice wet and hot against her ear. "Thank you."

"Sure. See you later." Sam hurriedly ducked inside the tent, her body thrumming from his embrace, her mind whirling from seeing Joi and reliving conversations with Oba.

That night, she sent him a text.

I saw your sister today, which you probably know. I didn't appreciate your threats about Trey. I don't appreciate your sister's, either. Back off, Oba. Let me rebuild my life.

His response? A smiley face.
Seriously?
Sam didn't bother trying to interpret what that meant. She forced her focus from what had happened at the fairgrounds to the three homes on the Carolina islands and what she needed to accomplish next week. Hopefully her text was enough to throw off Oba or anyone else from thinking Nick was Trey's dad. Either way, she needed to tell Nick the truth. Time was running out.

Twelve

Nick had planned to fly over to the Carolinas the day after Sam arrived. But other CANN business demanded his focus the first part of the week. It wasn't until Thursday afternoon that he boarded Christian's private jet and headed to the other side of the country. He told himself it was to see in person the 3-D images and photos Sam had sent over. The truth was, he wanted to see her. Just moments from landing in Charleston, he texted Sam of his whereabouts and invited her to dinner.

Dinner?

Yes. Landing in Charleston.

Charleston, SC?

Nick smiled. A slightly confused Sam was adorable.

Yes, beautiful. I have impossible-to-get reservations at a quaint spot with only ten tables. Highly recommended.

A minute passed. Then five. Ten.

Nick began to get nervous. That never happened.

Can't. She finally texted back. Contractors on the island. Problems. Call after landing.

We'll talk tomorrow. I'll be there at 8.

Nick was disappointed but of course he understood. He also realized he'd been highly presumptuous to think that someone with the type of deadlines Sam had could drop everything to skedaddle over to the mainland for a ridiculously expensive candlelight meal personally prepared by an award-winning chef. As for problems with construction, they were as common as dust. He'd worry about those tomorrow.

Knowing from Sam's photos that furniture had yet to be delivered, Nick had Anita arrange a room at a hotel, and set up one of the chefs who'd responded to their targeted ad for personal service on the islands to be at the house the next morning. He planned for Sam's day to start with a delicious, satisfying breakfast. No matter how busy the day was, she had to eat. Once those plans had been made, he forwarded them to Sam so she wouldn't wake up to a stranger knocking on her door.

"What are you doing here?" was her greeting the next day.

Not quite the warm welcome he expected but again, he understood.

"Good morning."

"That's debatable."

Sam looked haggard, as though she'd hardly slept. "Come here."

She gave him the briefest of hugs. "I know this is your baby, Nick, but there's a ton happening today. I can't believe that you'd arrive unannounced."

"It's good I did from the looks of things. Did you get any sleep last night?"

"Very little and thanks, but I've got this. I know how to call in reinforcements if needed."

"I wouldn't have hired you had I not thought you capable. I wanted to see you, okay? As Nick, not your boss."

Those words seemed to break through the wall of frustration around her. When he again invited her into his arms, she stepped in and squeezed back when he wrapped his arms around her. He kissed her cheek, eyes, forehead.

"Did the chef arrive?"

"In the kitchen."

"Hungry?"

"I could eat."

Nick looked around at the empty rooms.

"There's a railing outside on the patio where we could sit," she said.

Someone behind them cleared their throat.

"Excuse me, good morning, sir."

Nick turned to the chef in a signature white coat, his long locs neatly wrapped into a bun at the nape of his neck.

"Hi, I'm Nick."

"Gregory, sir. Nice to meet you. I've set up a bit of a beverage station in the other room. My instructions were to forgo taking personal orders and fix something amazing."

"That sounds like Anita," Nick said, smiling. "Thanks, Gregory. We'll help ourselves to the drinks and be waiting outside."

"I've taken the liberty of preparing a spot out back,

sir. There was a picnic table and benches set up. I hope you don't mind."

"Not at all." Nick looked at Sam.

"It's where the construction crew eats. Let's get our drinks and head out there."

They walked into the other room where Gregory had set up a table with coffees, teas and juices.

Sam filled a tall mug with coffee. Nick poured tea. Both grabbed glasses of orange juice, then walked outside to a beautiful, slightly humid day in the Palmetto State. The dusty construction area had been transformed into an idyllic scene. The area around the table had been swept of debris. White linen covered the table where a vase of wildflowers sat in the center of the table.

"Hope you're hungry."

"A private chef, Nick. I appreciate the gesture but seriously… I would have been fine with a breakfast sandwich."

"Each vacation home comes with a staff, including a chef. The guy fixing breakfast is on an audition of sorts for one of three positions on this island that will need to be filled."

"These magnificent homes and a private chef, too. I'm almost afraid to know the nightly rate."

"The smaller homes go for just under 10K, nightly. The price and amenities go up from there."

"Crazy that some people can spend in one night what could pay somebody else's rent for a year."

"Rich people are going to spend money, babe. Might as well be with us."

Sam held up her orange juice. "Touché."

While waiting for Gregory, they engaged in small talk about the weather, Nick's family and the kids.

"Speaking of, where is the young equestrian?"

"Back in Vegas with Gloria so that he can attend his cousin's birthday party."

"Sounds like she's working out for you."

"She's a godsend, and very good with Trey."

Once the food had been brought to the table, Nick returned to business. "I'm very pleased with the progress I see so far. Tell me about the problems you're having."

Over a superb breakfast that included crispy spiced chicken over fluffy pecan waffles, truffle-infused egg whites and mouthwatering crab cakes, Sam shared the challenge with suspending the bridge as her drawings had rendered, over a sizable koi pond. Later, they met with the contractor and with Nick's insightful suggestions, came up with a workable alternative. Sam loosened up. Nick spent the night. With Sam obviously having forgotten about them not repeating their sex romp, they christened the shower with their lovemaking, then cuddled in a twin-size futon, the home's lone piece of temporary furniture until the main shipment arrived next week. He returned to Breedlove spent and satiated, able to once again focus on work.

The day after returning back home and having put in almost ten hours at the office, he called his brother to hopefully shoot some hoops.

"Twin, let's ball," he said, once Noah answered.

"You're back?"

"Yeah, where were you today?"

"Working from home."

"How's Dee?"

"Better. The premature contractions stopped and there's been no bleeding."

"Whoa, TMI, dude!"

"Hey, it's all part of bringing another being into the world."

"I'm happy to leave that up to my brothers and be the best Uncle Nick in the world." Noah didn't respond. "That was a joke."

"When are you coming over?"

The seriousness in Noah's voice could not be missed. Had he caught attitude because of Nick's joking comment? Nick chalked it up to Noah being concerned about his wife and the health of his child. Damaris "Dee" Glen Breedlove helped save his brother's life once. Nick knew Noah would do all he could to return the favor.

Nick stopped by his place, changed clothes, then continued down the road, around the bend and toward the mountains to his brother's new home. Noah and Dee had designed it together, a combination of the styles Dee grew up seeing in Utah and the rustic yet modern touches Noah enjoyed. There were cows for fresh milk and chickens that provided Dee's preferred organic eggs, a pet pig named Rosy, two dogs, and a cat. Dee had changed his twin brother, no doubt about that. It made him wonder what kind of changes someone special would bring into his life. An image of Sam floated into his mind. Remembering there was no time in his life for that kind of special, he pushed it away.

He knocked on the door. Dee answered. "He's out back," she said, her hands dusty with flour.

"What are you making?"

"Pies, and yes, I have one for you."

Nick gave her a thumbs-up, then jogged around to where Noah was putting up free throws on the combination basketball and tennis court located several yards beyond Dee's garden. Anyone else would see a guy loose and relaxed, casually playing a sport. But Nick knew his twin almost better than himself. Something was going on.

"What's up, bro?"

"You got it." They exchanged a fist bump. "How was the Carolinas?"

"Hot. Humid."

Noah jogged for a layup. Nick jumped up to block it. Noah faked left, rolled around and easily laid it against the board.

"How's Sam?"

Nick couldn't help smiling. "She's good."

Noah stopped bouncing the ball. "What does that mean?"

"There are a few challenges but so far we think this build can stay on schedule."

"I meant the smile."

"Oh. That."

"Are you sleeping with her?"

"Wow, kind of blunt, don't you think?"

"Well, are you? I have my reasons for asking."

"Which are?"

Noah began bouncing the ball again but made no move toward the hoop. "Really, Nick, I don't even want to respond. It's all gossip, and you know how much I hate being a part of something like that."

Nick stole the ball and rested it on his hip. "What's the rumor?"

"It's about Sam."

Nick's heartbeat increased. Was she getting back with her ex? Was there another man?

"What about Sam?"

"And Trey," Noah said.

"Spit it out, twin."

Noah sighed. "I guess that's best. There's talk going around that the dude in Nigeria, the African prince, isn't Trey's biological father."

Nick began breathing again. Was that all? Since the

two were divorced that didn't seem so important; may have even been why they broke up.

"Doesn't sound like any of my business," Nick said, pausing to shoot three from the top of the key.

He headed over to retrieve the ball. Noah intercepted him and grabbed it instead.

"Word is the father lives here, in Vegas."

Nick shrugged. "I still don't see what that has to do with us. I hate gossip as much as you do. Someone obviously has too much time on their hands. Wait a minute. Where'd you hear this?"

"Lauren. She has a client who's opening a high-end boutique and travels in certain societal circles, the bougie crowd and whatnot. Said Sam's son didn't belong to the prince."

"Was the person who put this bug in her ear named Joi by any chance?"

Noah's brow creased. "Who's Joi?"

"Oba's sister. Sam's ex-sister-in-law. I met her last weekend at the carnival. Sam was with me and it was clear that there was no lost love between them."

Nick swiped the ball from Noah. "I wouldn't put too much stock into that kind of gossip, man. Come on. Twenty-one. Let's go."

"Normally, I'd say you're right. I wouldn't give those kinds of rumors the time of day. But this one is different, bro."

"Why?"

"Because of who they're claiming is Trey's father."

"Who?"

"You."

Thirteen

Sam woke up with a bad feeling, a complete paradox given she was working in what looked like a swampy paradise. She got up, made coffee and tried to shake it off. She called Gloria, texted Danni and her dad. Everyone was fine, yet the feeling persisted. She finally allowed herself to consider that the continuing angst was from the incident with Joi at the fair. The text she'd sent her ex and the reply she'd gotten. And how he'd gone radio silent since then.

What an impossible situation. It seemed that every major decision she'd made since that heavenly night she initially spent in Nick's arms had been less than smart. Not telling Nick that she was pregnant. Moving to Africa. Marrying Oba. Returning stateside to Las Vegas instead of LA. Taking the contract for CANN Isles. Not telling Nick about Trey after they began working together. Underestimating Oba's greed. Not telling Nick the moment

Oba threatened to do so, then sleeping with her child's bio dad more than once. Thinking that any of this would be easy, that Nick would somehow understand her betrayal. How could she think he'd be understanding when she was finding it increasingly difficult to justify her actions? At the end of the day, Sam had to face the hard truth. There was only one person to blame for what was happening right now.

Her.

Sam's mind settled enough for her to start the workday. Admitting her role in this mess, acknowledging that what she was experiencing was something that she in large part had created, was strangely liberating. In taking responsibility Sam felt some of her power being restored. She'd felt vulnerable after the confrontation with Joi, as though someone else had the ability to call the shots on her life. That was an illusion. It wasn't true. She'd made mistakes, but it wasn't the end of the world. Most importantly, the end result of that night hadn't been all bad. It had produced that which she treasured most in life. Her son.

For the next few hours, Sam focused on the home's furnishings—double-checking that shipments were still on schedule; confirming contractor appointments and speaking with the landscaping crew. Finally, she took a long shower and rather than heating up one of the meals left by the chef, decided to take the yacht into Charleston for a proper meal.

Thirty minutes later, she was at the boat's stern, watching the Atlantic churn beneath the sleek yacht's powerful motor. People often dreamed of a rich, carefree life where having a job or not was an option. Sam had lived that life, and until now didn't realize how much she'd missed her career. She was thankful for the tight timeline, and the plethora of problems to solve it presented. Doing so gave her less time to think about her own. And just like that, the sense of foreboding came back.

She knew just the person to help lighten her mood, reached over and picked up her phone. "Hey, Danni."

"Cousin! I was just thinking about you. It's about time you called. How's it going?"

"Okay, for the most part."

"I hope you're calling to say you told Nick about Trey."

"I'm going to. Soon. How was the birthday party?"

"Loud. Scott bought Jaylen a drum set. I wanted to take those sticks and beat him with them!"

Sam laughed. "I bet Trey was happy. I miss him."

"Hmm, I see. Do you miss his father?"

"Next question."

Danielle laughed. "Where are you?"

"Off the coast of South Carolina, heading into Charleston."

"From the island?"

"Yes, the island where the homes are located. They're super secure, super private and available only by boat."

There was a slight pause, and then, "How do you do it?"

"Do what?"

"Land these dream situations in your life. First, the marriage to a prince—"

"You had a hand in that."

"And now designing island homes for a rich guy? I'm doing something wrong."

"You're doing everything right. You've got a good man, a great kid and an amazing nephew."

"Ha! I can't argue with that. Hey, speaking of my nephew, he just ran down the hall. You want to speak with him?"

"In a minute. How are you?"

"Rested. That angel named Gloria who calls herself a childcare specialist is just the type of person I need in my life. She volunteered to help with the party and a few times since then, and made me wonder how I worked and ran this household without her."

"Frankly, I don't know either. Working full-time, taking care of a family and helping with Trey? I swear there's an S on your chest."

"Ha! I'm not your superwoman," Danielle sang. "Seriously, the workers at the day care are like family and my boss is a gem. As a single mother, she's well aware of the struggle in balancing family and work."

Sam looked out over the water, rippling and glowing in the sunny afternoon. Her cousin was right. She was blessed. Even with the design problems she'd encountered and her recent divorce, all the trouble she'd left behind in Africa and the secret she kept, life was good. She was on a yacht sailing in the Atlantic, having scored a contract any designer would want, one that would boost her résumé to the point she could be picky about clients and name her price. Her son was healthy and her dad was glad she was back on his side of the world. There was no room for complaints. At least, that should have been the case. But…that feeling.

"Sam."

"Hmm?"

"You got quiet all of a sudden. What's going on?"

"I don't know. I woke up with an eerie feeling that I've had all day."

"Was it a dream about Oba?"

"No. But something happened over the weekend that I didn't tell you about." Sam told Danielle about the run-in with Joi.

"And you're just telling me now?"

"I didn't want to even think about it, much less talk about what happened."

"Sam, you need to tell Nick about Trey. Today. The last thing you want is for him to find out about it from someone other than you."

"You're right. I know. I almost did that this weekend, too, right before Joi walked up and interrupted. And something else happened that day."

"What?"

"Nick and I slept together."

Danielle sucked in a breath. "No!"

"Yes." She painted the picture of them out riding, the spooked horse, sharing the saddle with Nick, and the inevitable conclusion from such close proximity.

"It was just that one time?"

"No."

"Twice?"

Sam sighed.

"You guys are working and dating?"

"Not officially dating, no."

"Friends with benefits?"

"You might say he's now a part of my compensation package." Sam's attempt to lighten the mood was an epic fail.

"You've got Nick hanging out with a child he doesn't know is his, and sleeping with him, too? Sam. You've got to tell that man the truth."

Sam's screen lit up. Her stomach flopped. "Well, Danni, looks like we talked him up."

"Who, Nick?"

"He's calling. I've got to take it. Look, I'll call you back."

"Tell him!" Sam heard Danni yell before disconnecting the call.

"Hey, Nick."

"Sam."

Uh-oh. Was it paranoia about her secret or was there an ominous tone in Nick's voice? It had to be her freaking out. There was no way that he knew.

"The one and only," she said with a forced cheerfulness. "If you're calling about the drawings, that'll have to wait until I get back to the island. I'm on my way into Charleston. Wish you were here to join me for dinner."

"In a way, I wish I were there, too. But I'm not sure I'd have much of an appetite."

"Why? What's the matter?"

"Earlier today I hung out with my brother, who'd heard a crazy rumor, that your ex is not Trey's father."

Sam felt nauseous and she wasn't seasick.

"Who told him that?"

"Lauren heard it last weekend, from a client she met."

Sam sighed. "That is not a rumor. Trey is not Oba's biological child."

"Whose child is it? Do I know the father?"

Sam closed her eyes, unaware of how tightly she squeezed the phone. "You don't want kids," she said, in what hopefully sounded like a teasing tone. "Why this sudden interest in Trey's dad?"

Nick paused for so long Sam thought they may have gotten disconnected. She glimpsed her phone's face. He was still on the line.

"Nick?"

"Am I Trey's father?"

There was a lump as big as the future in her throat. She swallowed past it. "Yes."

Silence.

"Nick? Hello?"

She looked at the phone again. Nick was no longer

on the line. Danni's words had proven prophetic. The secret was out and pierced her like an arrow. Straight through the heart.

Fourteen

Nick didn't think it possible to feel so many different emotions at once—shock, anger, bewilderment, confusion. He was Trey's father? Impossible. He went through all of the reasons that could not have been true. All but a sliver in the back of his brain was convinced that there was no way. But that 1 percent chance kept him from sleeping. The next morning, the sun had barely announced its presence when he walked through the front doors of the estate. Helen the housekeeper greeted him. She whispered, a nod to the early hour.

"Nick, is everything okay?"

"No, Helen, it's not. I need to see my parents."

"They're sleeping."

"I figured as much. They won't be for long."

Something in his voice must have warned her against making a fuss. Instead she asked, "Can I get you something? Coffee or tea?"

A shot of whiskey, Nick thought, but shook his head. One shot wouldn't be enough. This situation called for an entire bottle.

He reached his parents' suite and tapped on the door. "Mom. Dad. It's Nick."

"Nick?"

He heard the grogginess of his mother's voice, accompanied by shuffling noises, and felt a twinge of guilt, but only for a second. There were times when even a grown man still needed parental counsel. Now was one of those times.

"Just a moment, son."

Victoria opened the door wearing a floral lavender robe with a matching silk cap and heeled house shoes, the epitome of style even in sleepwear.

"Good morning, darling." She touched his face. "What's the matter, son?"

Nick hugged her and walked into the room, past the sitting area and into where his dad was leaning up against the headboard.

"Son?"

Victoria came in behind him and joined her husband on his side of the bed. "Nick, what's wrong? You've got me very concerned."

"You know Sam, the woman who's working with me?"

"Of course. You don't forget a woman like her."

Nick snorted. "You don't know how right that statement might be. After confronting her about a rumor, she blindsided me with the news that Trey is my son."

He watched his parents exchange a look.

"What do you have to say about that?" Victoria asked.

Nick began to pace. "I say it's impossible!"

His father, Nicholas, raised a brow. "Is it?"

Nick turned to look at him. "Yes!"

"You two have never been intimate?"

"A long time ago but—"

"How long ago, son?" Victoria asked.

Nick frowned as he did the mental calculations. Around the time Sam got pregnant, a thought he didn't share.

"He's not my kid."

Victoria moved from the bed to sit on the antique bench beyond it. "You're sure? You always used protection?"

"There's no doubt about that," Nicholas interrupted, confidently crossing his arms. "That's how I taught all my boys. To use protection every single time."

"And you did?" Victoria pushed.

Nick ran a frustrated hand through his curls. "There may have been one time…"

"Then there's only one thing to do. Have a paternity test taken and then go from there."

"Go where from there? I don't have time to be a father. I told her that these island homes are my babies right now."

"So you two have discussed this?"

"No. We talked about kids once and I let her know then as I've told every woman before her that having a child wasn't a part of my plans and still isn't…not for at least another ten years."

Nicholas eased out of bed, straightening his pin-striped designer pajamas. "Was that before or after the unprotected sex, son?"

"How old is her son?" Victoria asked.

"Four."

"Yet you're only now learning that he might be your child? Why?"

"I don't know!"

"Well, you need to find out. If the child is yours, you've lost four formative years of his life. He's missed out on being a Breedlove and we may have someone with our DNA that we don't know. All of that is reason enough for a conversation with Samantha. That girl's got some explaining to do."

The conversation moved from his parents' master suite to the breakfast nook where over coffee they talked for more than an hour. Victoria worked her mother magic. Nick left the house feeling infinitely better than when he arrived. He was angry with Sam, beyond disappointed in her actions, but because of the people who raised him, he would try to follow their advice and not judge her too harshly or prematurely. A hard ask, but he'd try.

Nick was in no shape to go to work. He called Anita and rearranged his schedule to work from home. Once there, he retreated to his home office but still couldn't work very much. His thoughts kept drifting to the possibility that he was a father. He could close his eyes and see's Trey's face, searched his memory for any sign of himself in it. He went back to the day that he met him, how he'd actually told Sam the adventurous child reminded him of himself at that age. He went over every detail of the day they went horseback riding. He replayed the showdown between Sam and Joi. Sam's behavior now made much more sense, as did Joi's comment.

Which one is yours?

She knew. Sam knew. Yet kept him in the dark.

And there was one more thing. Those anonymous calls he'd been getting from the blocked number and the person who never spoke. Did that have something to do with the secret that Sam had been keeping?

Nick spun around angrily, determined to focus on work. He fired up his laptop, gritted his teeth against the myriad of emotions and opened his email. His eyes were instantly drawn to one from Sam. Something about the build, he thought.

But it wasn't.

Nick,
I'm sorry. I wanted to tell you. I should have told you. I was afraid of your reaction. I didn't know how. Please give me the chance to explain why at the time I thought what I did was best for everyone. I'm not saying it was right. In hindsight, I realize it was a horrible decision, one not fair to you, Trey or me. Please forgive me. For everything.
Sam.

Nick didn't respond right away. He didn't trust himself to write an appropriate answer. Later that morning, his reply was succinct.

The only thing we need to talk about, besides work, is a paternity test. I'll schedule it and forward the details. N.

To say they talked that week would have been generous. While she was in the Carolinas Nick communicated through email and text. Dr. Lucas, a longtime family friend who could be trusted to operate in confidence, orchestrated the testing. It was he, not Nick, who contacted Sam, who swabbed herself and Trey in the privacy of her condo when they returned from the Carolinas. After swabbing Nick, Dr. Lucas personally delivered the tests to the lab and ordered the results be rushed.

Twenty-four hours later, all doubt was removed. Nick was a father. Trey was his child.

Fifteen

Sam had never been this nervous. Even while pregnant, while facing an uncertain future with a man she'd just met and carrying the child of another, her nerves had been less traumatized. Nick had agreed to come over to the condo so that they could speak in private. Trey was with Danielle. It was what needed to happen, and what she wanted. But that didn't stop another part of her from being scared to death.

She'd gone through her closet and changed several times. Finally, already mentally exhausted with frayed nerves, she pulled on a pair of jeans and a cropped tee. Her locs were pulled to the top of her head. She wore no makeup. She expected him. But when the doorbell rang she jumped from the couch, then paused for a deep breath. Was he angry? Hurt? Shocked? Resigned? The only way to find out which Nick was on the other side of the door was to open it.

"Hi, Nick."

"Sam."

The look on his face made her mouth dry. A combination of anger and sadness, disappointment and fear. That handsome face that was usually smiling was now almost ashen in its somberness.

She stepped back. "Please, come in."

He took a couple steps inside and stopped, his back to her.

"Let's, um, sit…at the table." Sam walked into the dining room and took a seat. Nick silently complied, barely meeting her eyes.

"Can I get you anything—"

"Let's get one thing straight. This is not a social visit. This is the opportunity you asked for, a chance to explain why almost five years later I'm finding out about someone out there with my blood in his veins."

He hadn't raised his voice, but Sam felt the restraint it had taken to not do so, could almost feel the heat on his words. Tears burned the back of her eyes. She dug fingernails into palms and dared herself to cry. She was not the victim here. She'd perpetrated a problem that now needed to be fixed.

"When getting dressed to go out that night, I had no idea how that party would change my life. Like you I was single and loving it, living life like it was golden, totally carefree. I think that's one of the reasons we gravitated to each other. We had the same energy, the same thought about living our lives.

"Discovering that I was pregnant sent me straight into shock, and panic. I'd recently ended a relationship with a guy in LA, had come here to get him out of my system. Boy, did you ever help me do that! As soon as the home test I took came back positive, I knew it was you.

But I didn't know you—I mean, we'd seen each other in passing what, maybe five or six times? Then I followed up with a doctor's visit and his timeline further confirmed it."

"But you still didn't tell me, Sam."

"I couldn't."

"Why not?"

"You didn't want kids! I'd gone online to find out more about you and the first article I read was about how dedicated you were to your family's business, how you were happily single with no time for a family of your own. Then, as fate would have it, shortly after that Danni got talking with Joi and found out about Oba's dilemma."

Nick's head shot up. "What dilemma?"

"Oba's elderly grandfather was pressuring his grandsons to get married and produce heirs. Oba was determined to beat Isaac having a child."

"Isaac?"

"His brother."

Nick's frown deepened.

"I know. It's complicated, the same as Oba and his brother's relationship. They were born less than a year apart. Their grandfather cultivated a fierce competition between them and upped the ante when he said the first one to marry and provide an heir would get the throne."

"How'd you get involved?"

"In a moment of frustration, Joi shared the stress of watching her brothers' ongoing fights with Danni, and how if given a choice she thought Oba would be the better king. Danni knew how freaked out I was at the prospect of being a single mother. She told Joi I was pregnant. Joi told him about me. Danni told me about Oba and…" Sam heaved a sigh. "The next thing I knew I was an African princess."

"That is totally crazy."

"In repeating the story out loud it sounds like pure insanity, but back then, in my mind, getting married solved everything. You wanted nothing to do with children, yet here was a guy where a child was not only what he wanted, but what he needed as well. I envisioned my son growing up royal and privileged, who'd lack for nothing he wanted in life."

"Nothing except the truth."

"There is no excuse for what I did. There's no way to make it right, only to make it better. For almost five years, I've deprived my son of his birthright. I will regret that decision for the rest of my life."

"I think your ex has been calling me."

Sam's head shot up. Her eyes registered fear.

"It was just a few times and I can't be sure. It was a blocked number. They never said anything. But since it's never happened before and considering what I've learned…"

Sam sighed and ran weary fingers over her eyes. "It was probably Oba. He's been trying to blackmail me."

"What the hell?" Nick had never been a violent man but he was glad Sam's ex wasn't anywhere close to him right now. "Why?"

"It's a long story, but don't worry. If it's him, they'll stop. Now that the secret is out he has nothing to use against me."

"Even with what you've told me, I still don't get it. How you could justify not telling me that you were pregnant? I don't know if I can ever get over that type of betrayal, the lack of trust, the anger. You watched me play with the kid, teach him how to ride a horse, and stayed silent while knowing I was interacting with my own son. That's fucked up, Sam!"

Nick stood and walked away from the table, as if just being near her was too much to handle.

Sam steepled her hands and worked to remain calm. "You're 100 percent correct. I effed up, in what may very well be the biggest mistake of my life. I don't expect you to understand something that no longer makes sense to me. I only hope that there can be some type of relationship between you and Trey and that one day... you'll forgive me."

"Of course there'll be a relationship. What kind of man do you think I am? Oh, that's right. You didn't think I was man enough to even want to know I had a child. So scratch that question. I don't give a damn what you think about me.

"I'm sure you know that if there was any possible way to pull you off the island project, I'd do it today. But given the time constraints and what has already been designed, it wouldn't be economically or logically prudent. That said, I can't be around you right now. Noah is familiar with much of what I'm doing. I'll bring him in as a go-between. All exchanges between us need to be electronic. In just over three weeks, the necessary homes will be completed. It'll be difficult, but I think I can handle the interaction for that long."

"What about Trey? I understand that you hate me right now, but I'm his mom and a necessary bridge between the two of you. Is there a way that we can at least work together to ensure as smooth as possible a transition for him, from considering Oba as his father to knowing you're his dad?"

Nick's eyes remained fixed on the window, though Sam doubted he saw anything beyond the mess she'd made.

"What do you suggest?" he finally asked.

"Maybe bring him over to the estate. He already loves going there. He really likes you, too."

Nick winced. The hole in Sam's heart tore wider.

"Maybe Christina can be a part of easing him into your family. I don't know what they think about all of this but…

"I'm so sorry, Nick." Instinctively, she took a step toward him.

"Don't." His jaw rippled with the force it took to not say more. Words Sam doubted she wanted to hear anyway.

"What about his nanny, what's her name?"

"Gloria?"

"Yes. She's friends with Christina's nanny Kirtu. I think it would be better if Trey came with her."

Ouch. "Okay."

"My family is understandably upset. They need time to absorb all of what's happened, as do I."

That night, Sam told Gloria about Nick being Trey's father, the conversation they'd had and Nick's request. The next morning Sam woke up Trey and helped him get dressed. That she wasn't going to be there for this first father-son interaction where Nick knew the truth literally hurt her heart. Still, she was grateful that Nick wanted to get to know his son. For that reason alone, she found a smile to put on for her child.

"Where are we going, Mommy?"

Sam looked at her heartbeat, melting as she always did when she heard Trey's voice. "You and Gloria are going someplace to have lots of fun."

"Where"

"Do you remember Nick, the man I work with, the one who taught you to ride the horse?"

"Yes. I'm going over there?" Trey's eyes were wide

and bright with anticipation. In that moment, to her mind, he looked like Nick's chocolate-covered mini-me. "I like horses, Mommy."

"I know you do."

"I want a horse, Mommy."

"That would be fun, huh?"

Trey nodded. "I would ride it every day."

"But horses are a lot of work, Trey. They require a lot of care, to feed them and house them and give them exercise."

"I'll do it!"

"Who'll watch the horse while you're at school?"

Trey's brows scrunched together as he pondered this question. Studying his face, Sam was taken aback. Why hadn't she noticed Nick's features before on Trey's face? Was it only in the truth being revealed she could see them?

"Are you going, Mama?"

"No, Mama's been working really long hours so while you and Gloria are riding horses, I'm going to get some rest. Is that okay?"

"Okay."

Sam would have liked there to have been a little push-back, to feel that her son needed her to tag along. But Trey had always been adventuresome, with an independent streak. Just like his father.

Sam heard a tap on Trey's bedroom door before it opened slightly.

"Good morning!"

Said a little too forced and a little too brightly. Sam could only imagine how awkward this had to be for her childcare specialist.

"Good morning, Gloria." She walked closer and lowered her voice. "Are you sure you'll be okay?"

"I still think it should be you who takes him over."

"Maybe next time. Right now, it's better this way."

"Should I fix him breakfast?"

"Knowing Nick and his family, any kind of gathering will likely involve food. I'll get him a Pop-Tart to tide him over."

Sam kept up the casual chatter until Gloria and Trey left the house and she locked the door behind them. She made it all the way back to her bedroom before the tears came, and then allowed herself a good cry. Trey would get to spend time with his father, even as Sam's days were numbered. She tried to find comfort in that.

For the next three weeks, a routine was established. Gloria took Trey to the Breedloves' on weekends. During the week they traveled with Sam, who buried herself in work. The good news was that for the most part she stayed on schedule, finishing the last home mere days before the occupants were set to arrive. The more challenging news was that she'd done all of this while consumed with a myriad of feelings about Nick and Trey. Delight that they were getting to know each other. Sorrow that things between her and Nick would never be the same.

The ice had thawed somewhat. The texts and emails had graduated to a call here and there, focused strictly on work or questions about Trey. She still wasn't sure how she felt about his reaction, that he'd been less than enthused about claiming the smartest, cutest, brightest most intelligent kid on the planet as his own. But in the end, as Danielle had so aptly pointed out, it would have been less than responsible for him to react any other way. His disappointment in missing out on Trey's first four years overshadowed the joy Sam was sure that Nick also felt. Whether he knew it, acknowledged it or ever owned up to it or not, Nick was a perfect father for her son. And thanks to the contract they'd negotiated, she would be fine financially and otherwise, whether or not Nick chose to be in her son's life.

She was in Maine preparing to catch a flight back to Vegas when her phone rang. Nick.

"Hey."

"Hi, Sam. You're headed back tonight, right?"

"Yes, headed to the airport now."

"What time do you land?"

"Seven forty-five."

"We need to talk. Can you meet me for dinner?"

Could it be that Nick was finally coming around to the two of them at least being friends for their son's sake? Sam's heart leaped.

"Sure. Should I bring Trey?"

"This needs to be just the two of us."

"Okay, text me the address and I'll meet you there. And, Nick?"

"Yes?"

"Thanks."

Once home she swapped jeans for a flowy jumpsuit and headed to Breedlove. Her phone rang. Thinking it was Danielle, she clicked the Bluetooth immediately.

"Hello, Sam Price," she fairly sang, her heart lighter than it had been in ages.

"Is that you, baby?"

Hearing the accent almost made her run off the road. Before Oba had only texted. Now he was calling. The nerve of his actions caused a rage to form in the pit of Sam's gut. That with all she was going through, he'd put her through more. But what could he do now? He'd lost his power. The thought calmed her anger. She almost smiled.

"Oba, we've been through this already. It's over. We've no need to talk."

"Oh, really? Then maybe you'd like me to talk to your baby's real daddy."

"Oba Usman, I don't give a damn what you do. There's nothing you can tell Nick that he doesn't already know. I told him, all right? He knows that Trey is his son. Call again threatening blackmail or anything else and you will hear from my lawyer. Think I'm playing? Try me. Now go off and have a nice life."

Sixteen

Having grown up in a nurturing, supportive environment filled with love, Nick wasn't used to being nervous. Yet as he pulled into the parking lot of BBs, his brother's popular hamburger joint, he felt wisps of discomfort, uncertainty, even a little despair. He'd always been the master of his own destiny, in total control of his life. Yet in the span of a few pivotal weeks that had all changed. He was a father. He had a son named Trey. Life was no longer all about him and while he'd already developed true feelings for what his brother Christian called Nick's "mini-me," he didn't quite know how he felt about that. Or about Sam.

He entered the restaurant, aware of the desirous eyes from female patrons that followed him only because the hostess pointed it out. After taking a seat near the window he pulled out his phone to check messages and texts until Sam arrived about fifteen minutes later.

"Sorry I'm late," she began, with a flustered demeanor. "There was an accident and…"

He put a hand on her arm and gently squeezed it. "Relax. It's fine. This isn't an interview."

Sam blessed him with a smile that lit up those warm brown eyes. "I guess you're right. Thanks for the reminder."

She sat down and threw her purse strap over the chair back. "This is your brother's place?" she asked, looking around.

"His pride and joy, except for the ranch and the cows he raises."

"I like its no-nonsense casual atmosphere. A contrast to what I imagined it would be."

"Adam wanted a place that would feel comfortable for everybody. Non-pretentious, as it should be when scarfing down burgers and fries. And speaking of, don't you dare say you're not hungry. I'd put these burgers up against anybody, and bet my vacation homes that they'd win."

"Wow, lofty bet."

"Confident brother."

They spoke casually until the server delivered their drinks and took their orders.

"A premium champagne would have been more appropriate, but such is not on BBs menu. This is all I have." Nick held up his frosty mug of beer. "A toast is in order."

With a slight frown, Sam held up her iced tea. "To what?"

"You. Congratulations on a job well done."

"Oh. That."

"I know the team congratulated you on managing the impossible. Noah, and my brothers. I think even my dad. I realized that no matter what was happening personally between us, not giving props where they were due made me a total jerk."

"It means a lot to hear that, Nick. It was the most difficult job I've ever tackled, and the most rewarding."

"To the only woman who could have pulled it off."

Sam lifted her tea. The glasses clinked. Each sipped from their glass as they drank in each other.

"We're having a dinner at CANN to celebrate the project's completion. I'd love for you to join me."

"As your date?"

"As one who deserves to be officially recognized."

"Are you sure? At our last physical interaction you hated me, Nick. This change, it's...welcomed, but uncomfortable."

"You're right. All I wanted was you out of my sight. Not telling me about my son was cruel and unthinkable. I thought I'd never forgive you."

Sam's head dipped. "I totally understand that, because I'll never forgive myself."

"Then I talked with Grandma Jewel, my dad's mother. She told me that the unforgiveness in my heart wouldn't hurt you or myself as much as it would Trey. That kids are closest to spirit and could feel words that remained unspoken. My son has already been through enough. I don't want to be the cause of more pain.

"One more thing," he continued, before Sam could speak. "Since I've done the impossible and forgiven you, you might as well forgive yourself."

Nick watched as Sam's head dipped lower, and she brought a hand to her face. He was out of his chair in an instant and sitting beside her.

"Come on, none of that," he said as he reached for a napkin and blotted her tears. "This is a celebration, remember?"

Sam pulled herself together, her expression über-serious as she turned to face him. "There's only one thing left to do."

Nick's heart skipped a beat. What had he missed? "Go ahead," he said. "I'm listening."

"We've got to tell Trey that you're his real father. He doesn't know that he's your son."

For the rest of the evening conversation swung between CANN Isles and Trey, mostly. The celebratory dinner took place a couple weeks later. Sam looked delectable in a designer original. Her good looks and effervescent personality endeared her to everyone in the room. Pics of her achievements were leaked to the media. In several issues of local and national newspapers and websites, she was the focus of both the business and society pages. No one was more impressed with her than his family. As though the person she was had overridden what she'd done. When Trey asked him if his mom was joining them for Thanksgiving dinner at the estate, Nick told him he'd like nothing better. The day marked for giving thanks seemed infinitely appropriate to being the one where his son learned the truth about their relationship.

Thanksgiving at the Breedlove estate was its usual grand affair. Nick and Sam, however, excused themselves shortly after the Christmas tree lighting, for a talk before Trey went to bed. He was excited from the day's festive activities but after Sam had given him a bath, he slid into his Black Panther pj's more than ready for sleep. Nick and Sam followed him into the massive guest room that had been renovated into a little boy's dreamland. Trey crawled onto the bed shaped like a race car. Nick sat down beside him. Sam, in the nearby chair.

Trey looked from one parent to the other. "You're both going to read me a bedtime story?"

"Not from one of your superhero books," Sam offered. "But Mama does have a story to tell."

Nick watched Sam take a deep breath as a myriad of emotions played across her face. "I know you think Prince Oba is your father, baby. But he is not your real dad."

Trey's look of confusion was understandable to both Nick and Sam. "He's not my father?"

Sam slowly shook her head. "No, baby. When I married him, you were already in my tummy."

Trey thought on this a moment and then asked his mom, "Do I have a father?"

"Absolutely," Nick interrupted, pride underscoring the word. "I'm your father, Trey. I only found out when you guys returned to America that I am your real dad."

He held his breath and watched Trey's young mind try to process adult information. "For real?"

Nick nodded.

"Like Christian is Christina's dad and Scott is Jaylen's dad?"

"Yes," Sam told him. "Exactly like that."

"Is that okay with you?" Nick asked him, unaware that he was no longer breathing.

"I love it!" Trey finally screamed, shooting like a missile into Nick's arms.

Trey's arms around his neck felt better than he could imagine. Nick finally exhaled. Sam didn't go home that night. The love shared between them was better than bliss. The work done. No more secrets between them. The next morning, she fixed them breakfast. Then Nick and Trey went riding with Adam and Noah. Family life continued when they returned and watched a movie.

The time felt so right, so natural, that Nick did the unthinkable when just before Sam and Trey prepared to leave that Saturday, he asked her, "Would you like to live here, to move in with me? Trey loves being here. There's plenty of room."

And other reasons, which Nick had yet to admit to himself.

Sam was understandably taken aback and didn't answer immediately. Nick understood. When it came to relationships, she'd gone through a lot. Yet his emotions surprised him as he awaited her answer, and at how lonely his home felt when he was the only one there. As he continued about his routine and enjoyed the rest of the holiday weekend, he knew one thing for sure. Even though the project with Sam Price was finished, the business between them wasn't over. Not by a long shot.

Seventeen

"Hey, cousin!" The front door had barely opened before Sam pulled Danielle in for a hearty hug.

Danielle stepped back. "What was that for?"

"Can't your cousin be happy to see you?" Sam entered the home.

"You're a little too happy. Where's Trey?"

"With Nick."

Danielle stopped and turned.

"For real? Even though it's not his weekend?"

"All the cousins were over playing in the pool. He begged to stay and hang out with them. With all I have to do trying to restart my business, I couldn't say no."

They continued down the hallway. Danielle glanced back a time or two.

"Somebody's holiday must have gone very well."

"Better than I could have thought possible."

Sam entered the living room and walked over to where her young cousin sat engrossed in a game.

"Hey, Jaylen!"

"Hi, Sam." Said with eyes still glued to the screen, his hand quickly shifting the control to combat and destroy enemies far and wide.

"Jaylen, take that warfare into your room. Mommy and Sam have some grown-up talking to do."

"Wait! I've almost vanquished the leader!"

"Vanquished?" Sam asked. "Good word."

"Boy, I'm going to vanquish your behind if you don't move!"

To prove she meant business Danielle walked over, picked up her son and began blowing smoochies—loud, air-filled kisses that tickled the skin. Jaylen's laughter floated down the hallway. Sam smiled, reminded of the roughhousing that Sam witnessed between Trey and his uncles. It seemed they were experts in everything from Adam and bucking broncos to Christian and any sport. Noah's collection of robotic toys had dropped Trey's jaw. Hers, too, actually. She'd never seen her son more impressed.

"Whew!" Danielle joined Sam on the chenille-covered sofa. "I'm too old to have a six-year-old."

Sam gave her a look. "You're thirty."

"Tell that to my body." Danielle shifted with a hand to her back. "That boy is getting too big to pick up. Now my back is killing me."

"That's because you need to work out."

"I need Gloria to find a twin to come help run my household, that's what I need."

"I hear that. She's been such a blessing to me and Trey, like part of the family."

"I'm teasing. That kind of help is above my pay grade."

Danielle shifted to a more comfortable position. "Enough about our angel assistant. It's time for you to spill the tea on all that happened in Breedlove. I want the turkey tales with all of the trimmings, thank you very much."

"Wow." Sam grabbed a pillow and leaned back, too. "So much happened. Where do I begin?"

"How about the beginning?"

Sam chuckled. "Good idea. You remember how incredible their place is, right?"

"They held a frickin' carnival on the most beautiful spot in all of Nevada, land that went on forever. How could I forget?"

"The holiday decor is even more spectacular."

"That's hard to imagine."

"Hopefully you and Jaylen will get a chance to see it. There were games and live music and incredible food. The night ended with a lighting ceremony that rivaled any I've seen, officially beginning the Christmas season. But I'm getting ahead of myself. The fun started with my meeting the true Breedlove matriarch, Nick's grandmother Miss Jewel…"

Sam recounted the unparalleled Breedlove Estate experience that for the past four days had been her enchanted life.

"You know I don't get along with just anybody. I can spot a fake real quick and don't suffer them lightly. But I have to tell you, Danni, the Breedloves aren't like most bougie folk. And I've seen one or two. Can we say 'royalty'?" Sam used air quotes.

"We could but we won't."

"Agreed. Nick and his family are different. They can hold their own with the caviar crowd but are down-to-earth, too. They're the real deal. I like them. The brother's wives were open, friendly, made me feel like family."

"Sounds like a family you want to join."

"Slow your roll, chick. That's unlikely to happen. Nick is warming up to being a father. The same doesn't necessarily apply to his taking a wife."

"I know you have to act as though it's not something that matters."

"For now I'm just happy we're getting along."

"That's all? No sex?"

"Well…"

"Girl, quit playing. Don't make me have to drag words out by consonant and vowel."

"I spent the night."

Danielle squealed. "That's good, right?"

Sam shrugged.

"Nick is one fine brother. You could do far worse than him."

"Look, I'm perfectly fine being sin—"

"Really? Then perhaps you should let your face know. Now back to the story before your nose starts to grow."

Sam burst out laughing. "I hate you."

"Thanks, hon."

Sam shifted the conversation out of the bedroom and back to the variety of activities that the estate offered, and how comfortable it was hanging out with members of Nick's family she knew already while meeting others for the first time.

"The brothers all have a natural affinity for socializing, comfortable mingling with others regardless of social status. The staff was treated more like family than employees. But I thought the family gathering, especially Thanksgiving dinner, would be different somehow. Haughtier, buttoned-up. I envisioned a dining room straight out of a castle with bone china, pristine manners and a servant behind each chair."

"What? No servants?" Danielle feigned indignation.

"Yes, but only behind every other chair," Sam deadpanned. "I'm kidding." Added a beat later.

Danielle bopped her with a throw pillow.

Sam's plan for a quick visit with Danielle turned into a chat-athon lasting all afternoon. After speaking with Nick, Jaylen joined Trey in Breedlove so that Sam and Danielle could take a rare spin on the Strip. Vegas residents seldom ventured to the areas that made their state famous, but Danielle felt lucky and Sam wanted to shop. When they returned to the estate that evening, the holiday theme was on full display. Danielle was as blown away as Sam thought she'd be. It was the perfect ending to her four-day weekend, and probably Sam's last bit of downtime before Christmas. There was work to do. Decisions to make. After a particularly wonderful evening involving the three of them, Nick had invited her and Trey to move in with him. Tempting offer. But he'd focused on Trey, not her or their relationship. She'd be the first to define herself as a modern woman, one leery of vows with a failed marriage under her belt. Still, she loved the security of commitment and knew few successes topped that of a good marriage. Seeing Scott and Danielle together was proof of that. Then there was her old-school grandmother's most popular saying that after being with Nick sometimes played in her head.

Doesn't make sense for a man to buy a cow when he gets the milk for free.

On their way home from Nick's after his offer, those words had played on a loop in her head. By the time she'd pulled into her garage, she'd made a decision. Sam and

Trey would continue to call the condo home. Grandma, 1. Modern woman, 0.

On Monday, Sam rose early. She'd created a to-do list the night before and was ready to tackle each project. She showered and dressed as if she were headed to an office. Sometimes a suit produced better results than yoga pants and a tee. Five minutes after sitting down with a mug of peppermint tea, her phone rang.

"Sam Price."

"Good morning."

"Hi Nick." *Breathe.* "What's going on?"

"Thinking about you. Thought I'd call."

"You're not working today?"

"Not for another hour."

"Oh."

Sam fell quiet, conflicted, as she'd been off and on all weekend. No doubt she was very attracted to Nick and loved being with him. Maybe a little too much for a casual affair. She'd played it off when Danielle teased her, but the deeper she'd examined her feelings about Nick and the more honest she'd been about the probability that they'd deepen further the longer they dated, the more she realized that continuing the casual affair might not be a good idea.

"Are you working? Did I interrupt something?"

Yes. You interrupted the lie I've been telling myself.

"Yes, I am working. There's only three short weeks until the world shuts down for Christmas. I have a lot to do before now and next year."

"Okay, cool. No worries. We can talk later today."

"Goodbye." Sam hung up and turned back to the to-do list on her computer. She tried to focus but her mind kept returning to her unresolved feelings about Nick. Getting up from the couch, she set down her tablet and walked to the window, her life over the past four-plus years playing like a video across a mental screen. The party. The pregnancy. Oba. Africa. CANN. Trey. The actions that had shaped her past. Her vision for the future. What did she want it to look like?

Determined to complete at least some of the tasks on her list, Sam picked up her phone and called Danielle.

"Hey, Sam!"

"Hey, cousin. Do you think the day care would mind watching Trey this afternoon? Gloria isn't here. I need to focus and right now home is too distracting."

"Probably not, but I can call and find out."

"Jaylen's there?"

"Yep. Scott will pick him up on the way home. He can get Trey, too, if you're not done with what you're working on by then. You can pick him up here later."

"Perfect. Let me know."

"Okay."

Minutes later, Danielle texted that the day care would watch him, but at the full-day rate even though it was almost one o'clock. Sam would have gladly paid them double. She was out of the house in less than thirty minutes and another half hour after that had dropped off Trey and was seated in a local library's private room with her tablet on and cell phone off.

The change of scenery helped but didn't squelch the thoughts completely. She managed to check off a few items and make the most time-sensitive calls. But three hours later, thoughts of Nick and their situation were still all-consuming. Her shoulders were tense with stress. Rotating her neck to try to remove the kinks, she remembered a conversation with Adam's wife Ryan, who co-owned a spa and suggested she should come for a visit. Maybe a little pampering was just what she needed to ease her body as well as her mind. After making an appointment online, Sam called Danielle to have Scott pick up Trey. She left the library and soon after arrived at the Integrative Healing Group, located in a nonde-script mall about fifteen minutes from the Strip. The place didn't look like much from the outside, but one step inside the red door that marked Ryan's business and Sam was transformed.

A soothing shade of blue covered the waiting room walls, with a backlit fountain as the room's showpiece. The water flowed into the vase of a tall, vibrant plant. More plants were set in floor urns and on tabletops. Notes from the instrumental music—something spiritual, earthy and from the East—seemed to wrap themselves around her, while the scent of lavender added to the paradise-like atmosphere. Sam looked around for the button that would announce her arrival and pushed it, as the confirmation email had instructed. It wasn't long before she heard the sound of bells, these tinkling as the door to the inner rooms opened and Ryan appeared.

"Sam, hi." Ryan stepped forward and offered a quick embrace. "I was so excited to see your name come up on our scheduler and actually moved a client over to an-other specialist so that I could personally attend you."

"Thank you, Ryan." Out of the three Breedlove sisters-in-love, Sam had most connected with Ryan, who never seemed to judge her after learning of Trey. She was ef-fortlessly attractive yet genuine and kind. Her heartfelt gesture made Sam like her even more.

"I didn't know what to expect when I pulled up out-side, but your place is truly beautiful."

"Yeah, the outside is pretty deceiving. But we put our heart and soul into the designing that went on inside, wanting to effect a certain mood and vibration that would immediately put the client at ease."

"You designed this?"

Ryan nodded. "My and my partner Brooklyn's souls are in every room."

They entered a massage room. Here the shade of blue was darker, contrasted against a stark white ceiling flecked with gold. Abstract paintings, angel statues and renderings of spiritual masters brought in an ethereal effect. "Ryan, I love everything about what I've seen so far. You guys did an amazing job."

"Oh my gosh, Sam, I appreciate your saying that. Nick brags that you're the best designer money can buy, so coming from you that's high praise."

So much for getting away from thinking about Nick. Then again, she'd made an appointment at the business of one of his family members. What did she expect?

As soon as Sam was ready and the massage began, so too did the questions.

"You're really tense, Sam. Working a lot of hours?"

Sam nodded. "Now that my contract with CANN is over I'm focused on rebuilding my company, Priceless Designs."

"That can be stressful."

"Yes."

"Because of Adam, I know that CANN's business is booming right now. I'm surprised Nick didn't have you stay on for other builds."

"It was discussed early on but a contract worked best. The last few years have been a whirlwind. I need time to regroup, focus on Trey and decide how best to move forward."

"I don't know much about what happened, but divorce is never easy."

"No."

"Nick seems to care a lot about you."

"Sorry, Ryan, I know he's your brother, but I'd rather not discuss Nick right now."

Ryan graciously changed the subject without missing a beat before ending conversation all together to focus on her work. She was skilled and thorough. When finished, Sam's body was as limp as a noodle. Ryan gave a short tour and explained other services. Sam scheduled another appointment for the works—facial, body wrap and float tank session—the latter of which she'd heard of but never tried. When they reached the outer door, Sam turned and hugged Ryan.

"Thanks for inviting me to your spa. I feel so much better and can't wait to come back."

"I can't wait for your visit, which doesn't have to be limited to the spa, by the way. If you're ever in need of some girl time or want to bring Trey and hang out at the ranch, you're always welcome. Just give me a call. The business card you picked up has my cell number."

"Okay. Thanks again."

They stepped outside.

"Sam?"

She turned around.

"I know it's not my business and you don't want to talk but if I may offer a bit of advice about Breedlove men?" Ryan waited and when Sam didn't speak or turn to leave, continued. "They are fierce companions who love as hard as they work. If you grab their attention, even fleeting, it's pretty amazing. If you're lucky enough to capture their heart, though, don't release it. You won't find a better man."

For the rest of the night, Sam's feelings remained scattered. She woke up to them cemented behind the strength of her truth. The desire at the core of her heart that until now she'd dared not think about, let alone speak. She was precariously close to falling in love with Nick and wanting more than the man was willing to give. She wanted a real relationship. She wanted love. Commitment. A forever man. Happily ever after was sometimes hard to come by, but it was possible. She believed she deserved to have the life that she wanted. And that true love was worth the wait.

Showering and preparing breakfast, Sam felt more grounded and sure of herself than since leaving Africa. The insecurities that had dogged her since the divorce were replaced by feelings of a woman who remembered who she really was—worthy enough for a man to want to put his name behind hers. It might be a while before she was ready to jump back into the dating waters. There was still baggage from the marriage of convenience left to unpack. But one thing was for sure. Whenever she was ready and open to look, she'd be highly unlikely to find him while rolling around in Nick's bed.

Later that day, after crossing off 75 percent of what was on her schedule, she didn't wait for Nick to call her. She called him. She needed to set things straight before losing her nerve or, after seeing that hard, toned body again, her will.

He answered quickly, his voice low and sexy. "I was just thinking about you. Again."

"I've been thinking about you, too, all day off and on."

"All good thoughts, I hope."

"It probably depends on how you look at it. Either way, I've come to a decision."

"Uh-oh. This sounds serious."

"I think we should cut out the intimacy between us and focus on co-parenting Trey."

"Okay." The word had only two syllables but the way Nick dragged it out made it seem to have more. "May I ask why you feel that way?"

Sam sighed. "I'm still figuring that all out myself. What I do know, what I recently discovered or acknowledged about myself, is that I'm past the whole casual dating thing. While Oba's and my marriage didn't work out and I'm not looking to blindly jump into another, I am looking for more than someone just to spend time with."

"Such as?"

"Feeling connected more than physically. Feeling that I'm not alone in the world, that someone has my back and will be there for me. I don't want to use the word *claim*, that sounds so draconian, but there's a part of being a woman that wants to be wanted, needed, loved, who wants to be valued enough by someone willing to acknowledge that she's enough for him, that she's all he wants."

"That sounds like the marriage thing you're not wanting to jump back into."

"Mine was mostly a marriage in name only, and I said blindly jump."

"Y'all didn't have sex?"

"We had sex. We never made love."

"And that's what you want. Love, not sex."

"Yes. That's what I want."

As she talked, revelations continued to pour into Sam's soul. Fear diminished. She was emboldened to stand in her truth. She wanted a real father for Trey and real love for herself. To have both was possible. She now knew that for sure. If she couldn't get the love she wanted from the father of her child, she'd get it somewhere else.

Eighteen

Nick tossed a stack of papers on his desk and punched the office intercom button with more force than necessary.

"Yes, Mr. Breedlove?"

He didn't answer her because he'd jumped out of his chair and stormed out of his office.

"What in the hell is this?" he yelled before reaching his destination. He tossed the report on Anita's desk. Files, pens and sticky pads went flying. "The revisions I requested are not on that doc."

"Oh no, Mr. Breedlove!" Anita hurriedly straightened the messy report papers, then scrambled to retrieve the items off the floor. "I absolutely made the changes and must have forwarded the uncorrected document."

"Find it. Send it," Nick growled, punching the air with a finger for emphasis. "Now!" Instead of waiting for an answer he marched back into his office and but for the hydraulics would have slammed the door. He continued to the window, his brow creased in a perfect bad-boy scowl as he shoved his hands in his pockets and tried to calm down. He wasn't angry about the report. He was upset at the restrictions Sam had placed on their relationship. Wait, there wasn't a relationship. That was the problem.

The intercom sounded. "Mr. Breedlove, I just emailed the corrected version. I thought I'd deleted the first one after it was revised. My apologies for—"

"None needed, Anita." He walked over and plopped into his chair, then spun around to face the phone. "I'm the one who needs to apologize."

"It's okay, Nick. There's a lot going on."

She had no idea. Then again, Nick suspected she'd had an inkling. Victoria called it Mother Wit. Plus, Anita had been with CANN for over twenty years, back in the days when Nick and Noah played Nerf ball in the halls and stole candy from the vending machines. It's the main reason he corrected her when she first called him by his surname.

"Call me Nick," he'd said.

She refused, wanting to give him the respect due an executive and, if his hunch was correct, boost the confidence of a twenty-two-year-old who was wet behind the ears. But when a bit of chiding or support was needed, she reverted to being the mother she was, with sons and daughters almost Nick's age.

"That's no excuse," he said after the long pause.

"Well, I know you're busy and want those letters to sign before end of day. So I'll get back to work. But if there's anything else you need or ways I can help relieve any stress, just let me know. Okay, kiddo?"

Nick smiled. "Yes, ma'am." He reached over to disconnect the call. "Hey, Anita. Got a question."

"Yes, Mr. Breedlove?"

"So we're back to that, are we?"

She chuckled. "Absolutely. Sir."

"Cut that out."

"What's your question?"

"I'm seeking your opinion as a woman, not my assistant."

"I think I can handle that."

"Is it true that no matter how independent a woman acts, she secretly wants companionship and…you know… to get married?"

"Are we speaking…generally?"

"Yes."

"Then generally speaking, yes, I believe that's true. Much has changed, with the women's movement, the rise of feminism and such, and some women are able to remain single and be happy. But I personally believe that deep inside most women, most people in fact, want to love and be loved, to have a partner in life. You're still young, Nick, and driven. But one day I believe that you, too, will grow tired of dating, and want something more substantial, more grounding in your life. Until then, have fun!"

"Good advice. Thanks, Anita."

"Anytime."

Nick went back to work. He perused the report Anita had corrected. Went to the meeting he'd mentioned to Sam. The hardest work he did all day was trying to forget about her and the decision she'd made. His fingers itched to tap her name on his phone, but he didn't. Until now he hadn't realized the easy flow they'd fallen into of talking almost every day. Mostly about Trey, sometimes with design or architectural questions. He'd grown used to regularly hearing her voice, and missed it. Then on Thursday night, as he left the office early to prepare for one of his mother's many social functions, his phone rang. Sam. Coming to her senses about her sex ban, he hoped. He'd had his share of women but when it came to his child's mother, he had to admit that their connection was different from those others. Special. At another level. He was a passionate brother. She was the first to match him stroke for stroke.

"Breedlove."

"Nick, it's Sam."

"I know. What's up?"

"It's about Trey."

So the call wasn't about sex, or him. He ignored a pang of disappointment.

"He's okay, right?"

"He's fine."

"Then what is it?"

"Is it possible that he can stay with you this weekend? Gloria is off for the holidays. As soon as my lease is up, I'm moving back to LA. I want to fly over there tomorrow, do some house hunting, speak with a few potential clients, stuff like that."

Nick's bad week just got worse.

"What's wrong with Vegas?"

There was a slight pause before Sam answered. "Nothing. However, the bulk of clients requesting my assistance are in metro LA. It makes sense for that to be my home base."

"What about Trey?"

"What about him?"

"Will he be staying here, on the estate?"

"Most definitely not."

"It's not definite at all, babe. I don't want my son growing up amid smog, gang violence, police misconduct, the celebrity culture. He needs to be here in Breedlove, where he can run, play, breathe fresh air and be a worry-free kid."

"He's my son, Nick. There's no way I'm going to be separated from him."

"Me, either."

"There's got to be a way we can come to a mutual agreement that will allow me to grow my business and for us to continue to co-parent Trey. You've got the plane, and money is no object. You can visit on the weekends and spend time together, just like now. There's tons of father-son adventures that you can have there."

"That wouldn't work."

"Why not?"

Because that would leave little to no time to work on us. The thought startled Nick. The truth unnerved him. Did he really want an "us" with Sam? The past couple months had been amazing. What about six months from now? A year? Five? He'd had his pick of women since the age of sixteen. Variety had always been the spice of his dating life. All of his brothers were married and seemed happy. Nick thought he was fine living single. He enjoyed the bachelor life.

"Because I don't want to be a long-distance dad. I won't let you take him out of state."

"You won't let me? You can't stop me. You may be his biological father but that's where it ends. Your name is not on his birth certificate. You have no legal rights."

"That can be changed."

"Where is this coming from? You've never seemed concerned about it before."

"You never before suggested moving Trey out of town!"

"You have all of the resources in the world and can see him whenever you want!"

"How about I set up an account to cover your flight expenses so that you can come here and see our son. Whenever, as you said."

"If you start a joint custody battle, believe me, you'll lose. There's no way a judge would grant that to a man who's known his son for less than six months."

"Whose fault is that?"

"Doesn't matter. The court will rule in the child's best interest."

"And you think that's away from an estate with over a thousand acres, with trees to climb and lakes to fish in? You think the judge will look unkindly upon an extended family that is successful in business and pillars of the community in a town that bears the child's grandfather's name? Don't bet on how a judge will handle this, Sam. Or on how hard I'll fight."

He heard a sigh and could imagine her pacing, running a frustrated hand through those gorgeous locs as she often did.

"Look, Nick. I don't want to argue. So far, you've shown yourself to be an amazing dad. I don't want to take away from Trey the opportunity for you to be a big part of his life. I also need to rebuild my business in a city that will provide an almost unlimited amount of potential clients. We should be able to make a decision that will work for all of us."

"There's an unlimited amount of work for you at CANN. You should come back to work here."

"I think that given the circumstances it's best that we keep our lives separate, except for Trey."

"I'm fine with that." Not. "As long as you remain here,

where I can see my son as often as I like, and where he can grow up as part of our clan."

"You're being unreasonable, Nick. Are you using this as a way to get back at me for not having sex with you?"

"Do I look like a brother who can't get sex?" He instantly regretted the words and hurried on in an effort to clean them up. "This isn't about us. It's about Trey. The best place for a young, growing boy like him is in Breedlove, Nevada. I'll understand it if you decide to relocate. But Trey stays here."

Sam hung up without saying goodbye. She was pissed, no doubt. Nick didn't blame her. He'd be upset, too. But he meant every word he said. So much so that he reached for his phone, tapped the face and then a number. "Hey, Chris. Quick question."

"Shoot."

"Didn't Barry's divorce involve a custody battle?" Barry Hammel was an up-and-coming architect CANN had snagged from a competing firm.

"A straight-out war, brother. The wife used the poor kids as pawns. Brainwashed them into thinking Barry didn't love them. Insinuated that there'd been sexual abuse. It was ugly. But he won in the end."

"He got the kids?"

"Joint custody, and a ruling that without his knowledge and permission, she could not take the kids out of state."

"Do you know his attorney's name?"

"No, but I can get it. Why?"

"Sam's thinking about moving to LA. But Trey's not going anywhere."

Nick exited the highway as he ended the call, feeling sure about what he planned to do. He couldn't control what had happened in Trey's life before finding out he was the boy's father. But he'd have a hand in everything that took place from here. That was for damn sure.

Nineteen

An hour later and Sam was still so hot from the conversation with Nick that she probably could have flown over there on her own steam, with Trey tucked under an arm. He was beside her in the passenger seat gabbing away, excited to see his father. And the horses. And birds. For that reason, she played nice. From the answer to the text she sent, Nick wasn't calm either. His response to the fact she was on her way over? One letter. K. She reached the estate and waved at the guard who opened the gate for her to drive through. She'd been impressed with these lands since her first arrival. Nick's words wafted like rings of smoke in her ears.

It's about Trey.

It surely was, which was why Nick shouldn't have a problem flying to California. A child belonged with his mother, and this mother was about to be in LA.

The best place for a young, growing boy is in Breedlove, Nevada.

She slowed around a curve and took in the landscape. Breathtaking, with lush green grass, sparkling lakes, animals dotting the countryside and majestic mountains beyond. Straight out of a storybook. Did she have the right to deprive Trey of growing up here? Maybe not, but she couldn't imagine not having a daily presence in his life. Was it right to request it of Nick?

I'll understand it if you decide to relocate. But Trey stays here.

The obvious solution was for her to accept Noah's offer and stay in Las Vegas. But could she survive regular contact with a man she wanted for the long term but would most likely never have?

She pulled into Nick's driveway. Memories assailed her. The Thanksgiving holiday. His master suite. The night they'd spent under the stars making love. Sam jerked the door open. There was no time for a trip down memory lane. She had a plane to catch. Trey got out of the car and ran to the door. Sam had hoped Nick would be outside. Easy handoff with little talk. He wasn't. She caught up with Trey and grabbed his hand as they mounted the twenty-plus steps to Nick's front door. The landscaping made for mind-blowing curb appeal, with its majestic waterfalls and towering trees that hid the five-thousand-square-foot man cave that Nick called home. A thought assailed her that was so unnerving she almost tripped.

Trey loves it here.

The door opened just as they reached the last step. Security system cameras, Sam surmised. He was at his home and could do what he wanted, but did he have to be shirtless, showing off the abs she loved to tickle with her fingernails? His hair was damp as though just out of the shower. He clutched a red towel hanging from his neck. He looked tempting. Devilish. Perfect for all sorts of sins. More images assailed her. She hadn't shared the details of that night with anyone, but she'd never look at a shower stall or marble bench the same.

Nick crouched to look Trey in the eye. "Hey, buddy. You ready to have fun?"

"Are we riding the horses again?"

"If you want."

"With Christina and Jaylen?"

"Sure."

"Yes!" Trey pushed past him and ran into the house.

"Trey!" Sam stepped around Nick. "Are you going to leave without giving me a hug?"

Trey spun around and trudged back toward Sam. "I forgot." The hug was brief and noncommittal. "Daddy, can I play video games?"

Nick nodded.

"Bye, Mama!"

They watched Trey race down the hall. Nick turned to her. "Hey."

"Hey."

The air pulsated with words neither dared say. Nick kept his feelings behind a hooded gaze.

"You coming in?"

Sam shook her head. "I need to get to the airport."

"Still going to LA?" He leaned on the doorjamb, cocked a brow, looked like a centerfold.

"Yep." Sam pulled the carry-on holding Trey's clothing and toys toward Nick. He reached for the handle. Their hands touched. Something akin to an electrical shock ran up her arm. It took everything within her not to jerk away. She played it cool, stepped back and headed down the stairs. She took a couple, then turned. "I'll be back Sunday night. Will text you on the way from the airport."

A short nod was his only response before stepping back into the house and closing the door. An uncomfortable feeling swirled in Sam's gut. She reached her car and hesitated before starting the engine and driving away. One of the clients she was scheduled to meet the next day interrupted her thoughts. By the time she arrived at the airport, the exchange with Nick had been forgotten. She boarded the plane and lost herself in 3-D designs.

Forty-five minutes later, the plane descended over the massive metropolis known as the City of Angels. Sam looked out at the imagery of the place she'd called home since the age of five, when her family left their Tennessee roots and chased her mother's acting dreams to Hollywood. It was a place she'd found a little scary but immediately exciting. Her family had settled in the San Fernando Valley. Sam flourished there. Her dad Marcus preferred country living. She'd always loved the city. Yet as the plane touched down and taxied on the runway, she felt strangely disconnected.

After securing a rental, she plugged into Bluetooth and tapped a number on her screen.

"Hey, Dad!"

"Hey there, babe. How you are you doing?"

"Good. But I'd be doing even better if you say you're not busy tonight and agree to meet me for dinner."

"You're here in LA?"

"Yep."

"For good?"

"Maybe. I'm meeting with two new clients and have an appointment with a Realtor."

"Is Trey with you?"

"No. He's with his dad."

"The prince is over here, in the States?"

The feeling of discomfort Sam had shaken during the plane ride returned and rumbled in the pit of her gut. Moving back to California wasn't the only thing she needed to share with her dad.

Marcus spoke into the silence. "It's a shame that child barely knows his grandfather."

"We need to change that. I'll bring him with me next time, promise. Where do you want to meet?"

"Hmm, there's a Mediterranean spot that opened up not far from here. I've been meaning to try it out."

"Text me the address. I'll meet you there."

Sam pulled into the parking lot of a restaurant anchoring a small strip mall. She spotted her dad's pickup and parked beside it. Inside, she saw Marcus right away.

"Hi, Daddy."

He stood to greet her. She melted into his embrace and was surprised to find herself fighting tears.

"You all right, baby girl?" Marcus asked after the hug.

Sam sat in the chair Marcus pulled out for her. "Life's a little crazy, but overall I'm good."

The first few minutes were spent perusing the menu while talking about family and mutual acquaintances. After they'd placed their orders and received their drinks, Sam felt her father's eyes boring into her.

"Why are you staring? Has it been so long you'd forgotten what I looked like?"

"Damn near." He shook his head. "Hard to keep up with that fast lane you're living in. I still don't know what happened with you and the prince."

"Just didn't work out, Dad."

"Was he violent? Did he hit you?"

"No."

"Was he a good father?"

"A great deal of his time was spent on royal duties. I don't doubt that he loves Trey, but he wasn't hands-on."

"I never understood why you married him in the first place. If you ask me, everything happened too fast. At least your mom got to see you wed."

Sam nodded. That her mom got to see her walk down the aisle was the best that could have happened.

"You came back from Africa, had barely unpacked your bags before moving to Nevada and now you're coming back here? Sam, what's going on?"

It was a dicey question. As far as her parents knew, Sam and Oba had met, fallen in love and enjoyed a whirlwind romance before her "unexpected" pregnancy led to a grandiose albeit hasty wedding. It was time to tell her dad about Nick.

"You remember why I moved to Las Vegas, to work on a specific project?"

"With the casino hotels."

"Specifically CANN International. It's owned by the Breedlove family. I worked on the project with one of the sons, a guy named Nick, whom I'd briefly dated in the past."

"Oh, Lord. Don't tell me y'all got into it and you lost a good job."

"No, the contract for what I worked on is over. But not me and Nick."

"You just got out of a marriage, honey. Now, I'm not one to tell you what to do but you might want to let your heart heal."

"Nick is Trey's father. He's my son's biological dad."

"Something tells me that for this story I might need something stronger than that cola I ordered." Marcus flagged down a server. "Miss!"

Sam gave her father the condensed version of what happened. Even with her father's questions, she wrapped up the story before the entrées arrived.

"What about getting more work down there, close to his father? It can't be healthy moving Trey around so much."

"There's more work here. Nick can visit often. It's a short flight. Plus, we'd be closer to you. Kids are fairly resilient. Trey seems to adapt easily. I think he'll be fine and you said it yourself, he needs to know his grandpa."

"He needs to know his daddy, too. The one he just met."

Sam thought her father would be thrilled about her move back to LA. Instead, having dinner with him brought up questions she'd thought resolved. When she boarded the plane Sunday night, however, her decision to move back to Los Angeles and reclaim her life held firm.

Sam arrived back in Vegas to a text from Nick to pick up Trey after Monday's preschool. She quickly unpacked her luggage and placed an order with her favorite Chinese restaurant for delivery an hour later. She turned on the water to fill the jetted tub, then walked back into the bedroom to undress. The zipper of her jeans was only halfway down when her doorbell rang. Sam looked at the clock and frowned. Surely that wasn't the delivery guy already. She'd just placed the order.

After rezipping her pants, she strode to the door and looked out the peephole. The man on the other side looked like a delivery guy. She opened the door.

"Yes?"

"Sam Price?"

"That's me. But I just placed my order five minutes ago."

The man reached into what she now realized was a

pouch containing several types of mail. He pulled out a large manila envelope and held it out.

She took it. "What's this?"

"Those are papers that required a personal delivery. You've been served."

The man hurriedly turned and began walking away.

"Wait, who are you? What?"

"Have a nice evening, Ms. Price!" he yelled over his shoulder.

Puzzled, Sam watched the man until he'd reached the end of the short hallway that led to her unit and turned the corner. She eased back inside her house, closed and locked the door. She surveyed the envelope the man had delivered, then walked over to her desk, pulled the mail opener from a cup holding pens, markers and other office items, and slit it open. Inside was a stapled document of several pages. She didn't have to go past the first one for her world to tilt. The bold, black letters at the top stole the joy from the weekend—the new client, housing prospects, reconnecting with old friends, starting life anew again.

Nick had petitioned the court for primary custody of her son. What would she do now?

Twenty

Nick walked into work Monday morning carrying a bag of guilt. He could only imagine how Sam had reacted when she got served papers from him seeking primary custody of Trey. He wasn't sorry for filing them. He had every right to be a part of Trey's life, to share an equal role in raising and shaping his young, sponge-like mind. He hadn't wanted to do it. His mother had suggested doing so from the time she learned she had another grandchild. He hadn't. There was no need. The arrangements he and Sam had agreed to worked for both of them. The less involvement the judicial system had in his life, the better. The conversation on Friday changed everything. Trey's living in California was not an option. Going from one home to another in the same town was hard enough. He would not subject Trey to commuting between states.

He'd barely fired up the Keurig in his office when

Anita beeped in. "Mr. Breedlove, someone is here to see you."

Nick sighed. "Send her in."

He didn't have to ask who. Today there was only one person who would arrive at his office first thing unannounced. Sam. She swirled into his office, a look of anger mixed with determination on her face, and threw the order at him.

"You have some kind of nerve."

"I had to do it."

"You did not have to do this. We could have worked something out!"

"We tried that on Friday. You want to move to California. I want to keep Trey here. It's an impasse I didn't see us getting past without third-party intervention."

"You will not get my child, Nick Breedlove. I will do whatever it takes to keep him with me."

"There's no place you can run to with him that I won't find."

"I'll fight you tooth and nail, and I'll win. You didn't even know Trey six months ago. Do you really think there's a judge in any state in America who would assign a virtual stranger as the custodial parent?"

"Any judge would once they heard the details of how I was purposely kept out of being a part of my child's life. And for the record, I'm no stranger to Trey. I'm his father!"

"I never should have told you."

"You should have told me from day one."

"We've already been down that road. You know why I didn't."

"I know what you told me. It doesn't change the fact that it was wrong to outright lie to both me and Trey, presenting another man as the father of the child you claim to love so much."

Sam's gasp should have been a warning that Nick was going too far. But the horse was already out of the barn and running at a full-speed gallop.

"If that's true, prove it. Stop making it so difficult for me to be a part of his life. Stop thinking only of yourself and think of what's best for him."

"How dare you!"

"The best place for him is here, in Breedlove. If you want to continue having equal access to him I suggest you rethink your relocation plans."

"I hate you right now."

"You'll get over it. Or not." Nick strolled over to where the cup of coffee that was now lukewarm still sat in its holder. He felt Sam's eyes boring into his back and considering her state of mind right now, thought he'd be better off not turning said back.

He walked to his desk. "You're the one making this difficult. Not me. I offered a solution. You weren't interested."

"Moving into your home so that we could play family? So that you could have the life of an adult while still acting like a kid who'd not yet put his toys away? How was our living together supposed to look, Nick? How would the whole revolving-door dating situation work out? And once I found happiness, which I am ready to do, where would he and I hang out? Oh, but wait. Your home is pretty roomy. Or we could expand it. Each have our own wing to do our own thing."

"Ha! I wish you would try to bring another man into my house."

"I'd do so the minute you brought in another woman."

The intercom sounded. "Excuse me, Mr. Breedlove?"

"Yes, Anita. My nine o'clock meeting. I haven't forgotten."

"Just checking. Thank you."

Nick reached for a folder on his desk, opened it as he leaned back in his chair. "This conversation isn't going anywhere. Neither is Trey. You need to decide what's more important. Your career or your son. It's as simple as that."

Sam said nothing for several seconds, just stared, eyes narrowed, hands clutched into fists. She took a deep breath, walked calmly over to where Nick sat, and slapped him squarely across the face. Then with head high and back straight, she walked out of the room.

Nick watched her exit, slowly rubbing the area she'd smacked. "You're forgetting something," he said as she reached the door.

She paused, then continued out. Nick's eyes returned to the court papers she'd left behind. If someone tried to take his child he'd have them taken out. Given that consideration, that all she'd given him was one slap in the face, he'd gotten off easy.

Nick finished the nine o'clock meeting. He returned to his office, packed his briefcase and stopped by Anita's desk.

"I'm going to be out for a while. If anything urgent happens, hit me up. Tell everyone else I'll return their calls tomorrow."

"Will do. Are you all right, Nick? When that woman left she seemed extremely angry."

"Her name is Sam. She's Trey's mom."

"Oh."

"We're having a bit of a disagreement. But I'm okay. Hold down the fort."

Nick got into his Bentley Azure convertible, popped

the top and sped down the highway. He was headed to the one person he could depend on in times like this. Someone whose advice was always spot-on, who gave it to him straight no chaser and suffered no fools.

Victoria Breedlove.

When he pulled into the circular driveway, he saw his father Nicholas just back from walking Ace, the newest family member. The long-haired Komondor with locs like Bob Marley, only blond, was a bit too friendly for Nick's taste and sure enough, the moment he saw him came bounding over, tail wagging, tongue hanging, ready for love.

"Hey, son."

Nick sidestepped the dog. "Hi, Dad."

"What brings you by in the middle of a workday?"

"Needed to talk with Mom real quick. Is she here?"

"No, son. She and Lauren left early this morning for an impromptu shopping trip."

"When will she back?"

"Day after tomorrow. They're shopping on the Champs-Élysées."

Victoria would choose this crucial time in his life for a Parisian jaunt. Exasperated, he let out a short huff.

"Something I can help you with, Nick?"

"I was hoping for a woman's perspective, but I guess you'll do."

"Ha! Come in. Let's have a cigar."

They walked through the spotless mansion and entered Nicholas's office. The stately room, with its high ceiling, dark woods and a lingering scent of premium tobacco, had a calming effect. Nick felt his shoulders relax as he walked over and took a seat in one of two high-backed chairs that had been imported from France and were purported to have once been in the royal palace. He watched

Nicholas pull down a box from the shelf, almost reverently, his eyes sparkling as he sat and opened the lid.

"New brand?"

"More than a brand, son. This is a happening."

Nick wasn't that into cigars but even he was impressed with the story his father told while carefully preparing the cigar to be lit. Learning about pre-banned Cuban and Dominican leaf-wrapped tobacco that had been soaked in the most expensive cognac created, and that only one hundred boxes of the exclusive brand were sold each year, made Nick eager to taste it. Once he did, he was even more impressed. People didn't spend five hundred a pop without blinking for one cigar for no reason.

The next few minutes were consumed in the ritual of cigar smoking, of enjoying the first puffs of the exclusive smoke in the silence it commanded. Nick knew his dad took his cigars seriously and waited for him to break the silence.

He blew out a puff and smiled at Nick. "Now, for sure, I've lived."

"It's amazing," Nick agreed.

"Okay, son, tell me why you're here."

"It's about Sam."

"I figured as much."

"And Trey."

A slight frown marred Nicholas's handsome face, an older, slightly more rugged version of Nick's. "What about my grandson?"

"Sam plans to move to LA and take him with her."

A slightly raised brow was Nicholas's only reaction. "What do you have to say about that?"

"I said hell no. Trey belongs in Breedlove. I tried to tell Sam that but she wouldn't listen. So I hired a lawyer. She got served papers last night. I'm going for primary custody."

Nicholas nodded. "Good for you." He tapped the cigar against a tray before placing it there. "What is your question for me?"

"Sam flew into my office first thing this morning, angrier than I've ever seen her."

"Can you blame her?"

"No. She was so upset that she slapped me."

"Is that all? Had I done something like that to Victoria I imagine she'd have come after me with something that held bullets."

"Mom wouldn't let anyone take us from her, which is why I feel bad for where Sam and I are now. The attorney and I discussed joint custody first. But that would involve an immense amount of travel for Trey, a disruptive school schedule, that every-other-holiday mess that would be painful as hell. I couldn't bear to put him through that and I will not live without being a part of his life. I didn't see any other way around it."

"You did what you had to do, son. I would have done the same."

"Seriously?"

"Without a doubt."

Nicholas's words were comforting and should have made Nick feel better than he did. He left the estate and headed to Adam's and a horse ride to further clear his head. He believed that filing for custody of Trey was the right thing to do. Then why did it feel so wrong?

Twenty-One

Sam stayed pissed for three days. She canceled a couple appointments. Didn't take calls. Except for texts to Danielle and her dad, calls from potential clients, and Trey of course, she didn't speak with anyone. The situation between her and Nick was too personal. She imagined that those close to her would be on her side, just as she assumed Nick's family had affirmed his position. In this instance, she'd seek her own counsel. After what felt like thousands of hours of thought, she made a decision and placed a call.

"Breedlove."

"Hi, it's me."

"Sam, if this is about Trey, I've been advised not to speak with you. Communication has to go through my lawyer."

"I've decided to stay." Silence. "Nick, did you hear me? I'm not moving to California. I'm staying here."

"What made you change your mind?"

"Trey. Not anything he said, but the decision became clear when I focused on him. I'd never deny Trey the chance of knowing and being close with his father. You were right. Breedlove is the best place for him to grow up. I'm not sure there are any affordable options for me out there, but it's worth finding out."

"I wish you wouldn't do that."

"What, move to Breedlove?"

"No, spend unnecessary money. I know you don't want to live with me, but there are guest homes available on the estate."

"I appreciate that, Nick, but that would be too close for my comfort. I care about you," she continued, voicing a truth she hadn't planned to share. "Not just as Trey's father, but as someone for whom I have a deep attraction. But you've made it clear that there's no chance for a real relationship. So I need to put myself in the position to attract the love I want. It's the most beautiful place I've ever set eyes on, but your family estate is not that place."

"I can understand that."

A major declaration and that's all he could say? Sam wasn't sure he understood at all. In fact, she'd place a CANN casino bet that he hadn't a clue she'd fallen in love with him.

"What are you doing later? Perhaps we can get together over dinner and discuss how to do what's in Trey's best interest from here on out."

"I can do that."

"What about seven? I'll book one of the private rooms and—"

"I'd rather we meet in a neutral location."

"Fair enough," Nick replied without hesitation. "You choose the spot."

"I'll text it."

"See you then."

After making arrangements to drop off Trey at Danielle's house, she texted Nick the address to her favorite Indian restaurant, walked into her closet and began the search for the perfect negotiation-wear. There was no mistaking the mission. This would be a negotiation. Sam needed to convince Nick to withdraw the papers requesting primary custody of Trey. She'd also like to increase the amount of time Trey and Nick had together; to work out something more regular than every other weekend and "whenever he was available or felt like it" they'd established just after Nick learned he was a dad. She wanted them to come to a place where if not being friends, they could at least be friendly. Sam didn't want Trey to grow up with them fighting, with him in the middle feeling that he had to choose. Sam wanted a lot.

She aimed to dress for success in this meeting with Nick. It was an interview of sorts, the most important one to date in her life. Jeans were out, as was a casual maxi or anything too sexy. Nick would perceive that as a ploy for favor or worse, a mixed signal of what she wanted. Her bed became littered with unacceptable choices. Her hand finally touched the perfect item—a grape-colored knee-length number that complemented her curves without squeezing too tightly. She pulled her locs into a loose topknot and left a few tendrils to hang around her face and neck. Swarovski crystal earrings and necklace were her only jewelry pieces. They matched the blinged-out slingbacks she chose to finish off the look. Makeup was minimal but the grape-colored matte MAC made her lips pop. A spritz of cologne and she was ready for her close-up.

There was little traffic. Sam arrived at the restaurant

with ten minutes to spare. She parked, went inside and sat at the bar. Maybe a glass of chilled chardonnay would help calm her nerves.

A young bartender with a shock of red hair ambled over, slowly wiping the bar as he neared. "What can I get for you, pretty lady?"

"A glass of white wine, please."

The bartender rattled off a list of options. Sam settled on one and ordered the drink. Seconds later the door to the establishment opened again and all Sam could think was that a god had strolled in. Nick, looking incredible. Literally, good enough to eat. He wore black. Black suit, black shirt beneath it, black shoes. His face was clean-shaven, his hair newly cut. A diamond stud sparkled in one ear. Sam didn't even bemoan her body's reaction. The way her nipples pebbled and her inner walls clenched. For a woman not to react to a brother that fine she'd have to be blind. Or dead.

He approached her with a leisurely stroll and a hint of wariness in his eyes. "Good evening."

Sam gave a cool nod warmed by a soft smile. "Nick. How are you?"

"I'm okay." She felt him relax. "You look nice."

"Thank you." He looked better than nice, greater than amazing and finer than wine. Sam kept that opinion to herself.

The waiter returned. "Your chardonnay, ma'am." He looked at Nick. "What can I get for you, sir?"

"I'll order from the table." Then to Sam. "Shall we?"

The server led them to a corner booth of a spacious dining room. The stark linen, dark carpet and dim lighting made for a romantic ambiance. The smell of Nick's cologne that wafted past Sam's nose as she walked beside him made her work to remember that this was basically a business meeting. Definitely not a date. She wished it were. After they'd ordered and the server had gone, Sam spoke up.

"I'd like to start this conversation off with an apology. I can't remember ever being as angry as I was that day in your office but it doesn't excuse my behavior. I should not have slapped you. I'm sorry."

"I think both of us could have said or done things differently. I accept your apology and offer mine as well. There has never been any doubt in my mind that Trey comes first in your life. For me to suggest otherwise may have warranted a slap. And for the record, woman, you pack a mean palm."

"I've never hit anyone in my life. Losing my temper like that was not cool. The suggestion that I would put work before Trey cut deeply. But hearing that caused me to take a step back as well. It made me become unflinchingly honest with myself and the real reasons behind my decision to move back to LA."

"Something besides it being a bigger, better market with more potential for work?" Nick reached for his water glass.

"Yes." Sam's chin lifted a bit as she said, "I was relocating to get away from you."

Nick almost spewed out his drink. "Whoa!"

"Too honest for you?" Sam shrugged. "It's all I've got. I figure being as honest as possible is the only way to move forward, the only way we can develop an authentic relationship where we get along. Again, for Trey's sake."

"How was I responsible for you wanting to move?"

Sam gave him a look. "You have no idea?"

Were men really that stupid?

"You want to get married but... I'm not ready for that."

"I know. That's the problem. It's difficult for me to be

around you and not…want to be with you. Yet it's hurtful to be with you intimately and know that's all it is."

"That's all it was the night we met. We were practically strangers."

"Which is why it was easy. My heart wasn't involved."

Nick eased back against the booth, sipped his water. No response. Sam figured it was just as well. Since he wanted to continue to sow his opulent oats, what was there to say? She decided it was time to stop talking about the "we" that wasn't and focus on why they were there.

"About Trey…"

He leaned forward, steepled his hands, engaged again. "Yes."

"I'd like you to withdraw your case for primary custody."

"Done."

Sam didn't try to hide her surprise. "Really? That simply? What's the catch?"

"No catch. I'll no longer seek primary custody. However…"

"Ah, here we go."

"Wait. Hear me out. I'm not a fan of the judicial system involving themselves in family matters unless absolutely necessary. We're intelligent people who both love Trey and want the best for him. I think we should be able to work out a mutually agreeable joint custody arrangement, one that will be drawn up by my attorney—"

"So much for no judicial involvement."

"This is legal involvement, an officially written position on what we both decide is best for Trey. It holds us accountable and in the case of another major disagreement would prevent either party from doing something crazy."

"Oh, so you're calling me crazy?" The twinkle in

Sam's eye let Nick know she was teasing. The atmosphere lightened, a little.

"Not at all, though you did marry a prince you barely knew and move to the other side of the world. It's not a stretch to believe you could change your identity and appearance and go on the run with my kid."

Sam put a finger to her chin. "Hmm. Ideas."

"Woman, don't you dare."

"I wouldn't."

"There's not a place on earth you could hide with Trey. I can't imagine him not being in my life."

"Me either. Drawing up a legal document is reasonable, I guess. That way neither could change our mind and go off on a tangent."

"There's one more thing."

"What?"

"I want my name on Trey's birth certificate."

"Done, and we can change his last name."

"Really? That simply?"

"Stop mocking me."

"Hard to do. You're so pretty with a chagrined face."

"A chagrined face? Is that supposed to be a compliment? You'd better be glad your looks get you women because your flirt game needs work!"

Dinner was served. Nick and Sam fell back into the easy camaraderie that marked their being together when not fighting like cats and dogs. Over the next ninety minutes they worked out a schedule that suited them both. Because he was often busy weekdays, Sam agreed for Nick to have Trey every weekend, with wiggle room for special events or celebrations when Sam would want Trey with her. During the week, with advance notice, he could stop by and visit Trey, or take him out for dinner or to the estate. Nick understood how important it was for Trey to bond with Sam's father, and would give up a weekend or two if Sam was scheduled to be in LA. They discussed a few more particulars such as schooling, doctor appointments and male bonding during haircuts.

"One last thing."

Sam's fork stopped in midair. "You said that about the birth certificate."

"Okay, this is the last of the last thing." He paused to finish his bite. "I want you to move to Breedlove."

"If things were different it would be a dream come true. The place is like paradise. But we've already discussed this, Nick. I don't want to live on the estate."

"I know. You've made that painfully clear. So I called up a buddy of mine and asked about properties around town. Turns out there's a three-bed, two-bath place near the town center that just became available. It's small, less than two thousand square feet, and is a bit unfinished. I told him you were a designer and not to worry about that. It might be better that there's work to be done. You can put your own stamp on it."

"What's the asking price?"

"Don't worry about it. I'm buying it for Trey. I'm doing what I wasn't able to for the first four years of his life—be financially responsible. Take care of him."

It was a position Sam couldn't argue.

"So how does that work? The house would be in his name?"

"He's not old enough to own it legally until he's eighteen. I've established a trust for him. If you both like it and want to move, the home will be bought in his name through the trust."

"Good to know I get some say in it," Sam teased.

"Of course. He sent me a picture of the outside. Would you like to see it?"

"Sure."

Nick tapped his screen, scrolled a bit and then handed his phone to Sam. The home was nothing like the simple abode she imagined. On the outside at least it was stunning, a contemporary Craftsman, with what looked to be sweeping city and mountain views, and large windows across two-story ceilings that she imagined let in lots of natural light.

"If you'd like I can give you his number. You two could take it from there, let me know what you think."

Sam nodded. "Okay. This doesn't mean that for sure I'll move there but it's worth checking out."

Dinner ended. Nick and Sam went their separate ways. Her mind reeled with the implications of Nick buying the home where she and Trey would reside. She didn't know how she felt about that but damn if it didn't feel good hanging out with him again.

Twenty-Two

Nick bopped up the stairs and tapped a tune on his twin's doorbell before opening the door and walking inside.

"Yo, No!"

He continued past the impressive foyer and down the hall in Noah's new home. "Noah!"

Noah's expecting wife Damaris rounded the corner. "Wow, you're up early."

"A lot to do. Where's Noah?"

"Swimming."

Since facing health challenges the year before, Noah had taken to daily swims to keep his body toned and his back muscles limber. He and Damaris had built a stunning home near the estate's mountain range and included an indoor pool with a retracting roof for an outdoor feel in the summer months. It was a stunning construction, a clever mix of the English Tudor style popular in Damaris's home state of Utah and the clean, simplistic yet ultramodern look common in the Scandinavian country of Denmark, where Noah and Damaris traveled several times a year.

Nick bent his face to Damaris's stomach. "Hello, nephew!" He held the greeting as an echo.

Damaris laughed. "You mean niece."

"You'll have a son, trust me. Ask my mom," Nick threw over his shoulder as he proceeded toward the home's north wing that along with the pool contained a full-size exercise room, sauna and game room. "It's the Breedlove way."

He reached the pool. It was empty. "Twin!"

Noah came out of the shower, wiping off with a fluffy white towel. "It must have worked." He pulled on a pair of long shorts.

"What?"

Noah's lips eased into a smile. "Yeah, it worked. Sam's moving into the house."

"I'm pretty sure of it. Larry called last night. She made an appointment for a walk-through first thing today."

"I think you're on the hook, twin."

Nick turned to Noah. "What do you mean?"

"You know what. I think Sam has caught a big fish. You look like a man in love."

"I'm a father who wants a secure life for his son."

"And the son's mother. Don't even try to lie. That smile is too big for one little boy, even one with your DNA."

Nick didn't answer. The twin thing. When one of their hearts beat the other could feel it. No doubt Noah could feel the seeds of love for Sam that had been steadily growing in Nick's heart since before he even realized.

Noah began walking toward the main part of the house. Nick fell into step beside him.

"You're feeling pretty good about yourself, aren't you? By the way, you're welcome."

Nick gave Noah a playful punch. "I'll give credit where it's due. Sam would have never accepted a home I purchased for her outright.

"Going from the Trey angle worked perfectly. What mother would deny their son a beautiful place to live?"

"Not a smart one."

"Sam's very smart." Nick winked.

"Beautiful, too."

"Man, don't remind me. She showed up last night with a dress that hugged her body the way I wanted to do. Locs caressing her neck. Skin showing, eyes glowing. Damn!"

They reached the kitchen. Damaris had prepared a smoothie and handed it to Noah.

"Thank you, baby." Noah gave his wife a quick kiss.

"You want one, Nick?"

"No, I'm good."

"We'll be in the office, baby."

"Remember, love, the doula comes at ten. Will you join us?"

"Yes, Dee. I'll be there to learn all I need to know about helping bring my son into the world."

Damaris chuckled as she shook her head. "You two."

The men continued down the hall into Noah's office.

"You not going to work today?"

Noah shook his head. "Working from home, bro. That's the good thing about Utah being virtual. I can monitor everything from the central control center."

Noah referred to a layout in the next room that gave him the ability to see everything happening in CANN's Mountain Valley, Utah location, where Noah had done the impossible and brought gambling to the state.

"All right then, man. I'd better let you get to it." Nick walked over and gave his twin a shoulder bump and fist tap.

"You heading to the office, or over to your lady's new home in Breedlove?"

"She's not my lady."

"Not yet, but from the look in your eye when you talk about her...she will be."

Nick didn't answer his brother, but long after he'd left the house, slid into his fancy ride and headed toward the Strip, what Noah said stayed on his mind. Did he want Sam to be his lady under the terms she presented? Truth of the matter was he hadn't been with another woman since he and Sam reconnected. But he was only twenty-seven. Was he ready to commit to being a one-woman man for the rest of his life?

Once in the office his mind was quickly pulled elsewhere. A private island in the Seychelles that Christian and Nick had their eyes on for over a year had just come on the market. It was one of less than half a dozen large enough to hold the type of opulent casino hotel they wanted to construct, one that included individual tiki-type houses that would sit directly over the water. Both knew they had to act fast to secure the deal.

Anita buzzed him. "Boss, Silver State Bank is on line one."

"Thanks, Anita." Nick tapped the line. "Breedlove."

"Nick, good morning. It's Harold. How are you doing?"

"Any day is good that starts out with a call from the bank president."

The two men conversed about the hundreds of millions needed for the Seychelles project, and how they would go about positioning funds that would be used by a variety of parties across continents. They scheduled a meeting among all necessary players for later that week. Afterward, the chat turned more social. Updates on family, plans to play golf. Nick's phone pinged with a text from Larry. He wrapped up the call.

"Harold, I have to run. Nice talking to you, buddy. See you soon." He hung up the landline and returned the call to the real estate agent from his cell. "Larry, talk to me."

"Sold!"

"Ha! She liked it, huh?"

"Are you kidding? She loved it."

Nick stood and walked to the window. The smile on his face could have replaced the sun. Having worked with Sam on the CANN Isles projects, he'd gained valuable insight into her tastes and design aesthetics. He knew she'd love the high ceilings, the myriad of windows and the open layout. Everything installed was high-end, yet there was enough left unfinished for Sam to stamp it with her signature style. He couldn't wait to see what she did with the place. Not that he felt she'd invite him over. But he'd have to go there to pick up Trey. The child that he never thought he wanted was becoming ever more intertwined in his life, and either directly or indirectly leading him toward a certain destiny. And though he wasn't quite ready to admit it, even to himself, Sam's stock was rising, too.

Later that night, as he was thinking about her, Sam called.

"Are you sure you didn't have anything to do with selecting that house?" she asked.

"Why would you think that?"

"The backyard is a boy's paradise."

"I heard there was a rock-climbing wall," was Nick's noncommittal answer. "I think Larry also mentioned that it was open concept as well."

"We… Trey loves the house."

"Great. I'll put in an offer tomorrow."

The home had already been purchased but Nick had to follow the charade all the way through.

"I'm still grappling with the fact that you're buying the house."

"I understand. But it's an investment for Trey. When he becomes an adult he'll have a place to stay, or an investment opportunity. If the market continues to move in a favorable direction and the city expands outward, the price of that home could double or triple in the coming years."

"It's an amazing gift for him, Nick. Having a home and with it financial stability at such a young age. Thank you."

"You're welcome."

Nick got the impression she wanted to say more. But she didn't.

"Like I said, I'll get with Larry tomorrow to put in an offer. When is the lease up on your condo?"

"Month after next."

"Will that be enough time for you to get the home ready?"

"I think so, if I can get the right help."

"CANN has a healthy Rolodex of contacts—electrical, flooring, installation, landscaping. We have established accounts within all of construction. I'll give you a card to get whatever you need."

Again. Silence.

"For Trey."

"Yeah, okay."

"I'll be speaking with my attorney later this week, to have him draw up the papers we discussed."

"You mean that you demanded?"

"Demanded is a rather harsh way of putting it, don't you think?"

"Do I have a choice in whether or not to participate?" Nick didn't have a comeback. "As I thought. I believe demand is perfect."

"Sam…"

"It's okay. I'm sorry. It's been a long day."

"Do you want to talk about it?"

"No."

"Listen, I don't want the legalities of my involvement in Trey's life to become a problem between us."

"It won't. I understand why you're doing what you're doing."

"But you don't agree with it."

"I wish it wasn't necessary but considering the circumstances and not knowing what tomorrow will bring, I guess it is."

Nick stretched out on the couch, feeling a strange yet definite comfort having Sam's voice in his ear.

"The document will only outline what we previously discussed. I want you to feel comfortable with what you're signing. So I'll have a draft version sent over to you before we lock in the wording. If you find a problem, let me know. We'll work it out. The attorney drafting this is Coleman Hughes. I can send his number as well, so you can ask any questions you have directly."

"I appreciate that."

"See how easy life is when we get along?"

"Bye, Nick."

Said sternly yet softly, in a way that made Nick feel all warm and sticky inside.

"Bye, Sam."

Nick watched a bit of television before retiring to bed. He lay awake for a long time, thinking about his dating life, trying to recall the women who'd most affected his life. There'd been more than a few but for the life of him Sam's was the only face that came to mind.

Twenty-Three

Sam's professional life was in chaos but thanks to Nick, the personal side was easy breezy. Diving into Trey's home's renovation brought the joy she felt these days. As for her son, she'd never seen Trey so happy. Every afternoon after preschool when they went to the home, he was out of his seat almost before the wheels stopped turning. The backyard was already his unspoken domain. The construction team had surprised both of them with a customized wood-and-steel fort-styled playground with holes for play shootouts and an enclosure to take cover. There was a slide and swings and beyond those, a sandbox. Behind it was a mini-trampoline. Sam was sure that Trey could live out there until he was a teenager and except for meals and bathroom breaks be perfectly fine.

"Sam!"

Danielle's voice bounced throughout the largely empty rooms.

"In the bedroom!"

"Which one?" Danielle said, with a laugh.

"Master."

Danielle stepped into Sam's favorite space. "Ohmygoodness! Look at your chandelier and ceiling fan combo. Just like you wanted. Where did you find it?"

"What I envisioned wasn't out there. I had it designed."

"Looks like it cost a fortune. Are the blades glass?"

"It's the next level up from PC, polycarbonate plastic. It's lighter and more durable than glass."

"I love the shape, like a sexy octopus."

"Now that you mention it, there is a resemblance."

"The way the crystals sparkle and play off the shiny stainless steel is just stunning. It's like magic. Every time I come over there's something beautiful and new."

Sam slid her hands into her jeans back pockets and looked around. "I have to admit, it's all coming together nicely."

"Nicely is an understatement. Sam, this place is amazing. It's perfect for you and Trey. Does it have a dimmer?" Sam nodded. "For those oh-so-romantic nights."

"With who, the hero from my latest Reese Ryan?"

"No." Danielle laughed at Sam's recent fixation with romance novels and her new favorite author. "Your baby daddy. I don't know when you're going to stop acting like a virgin and holding this all-or-nothing position. You love him."

"I never said that."

"Don't have to." Danielle spread her arms to take in the room. "Obviously he feels some kind of way about you. He's not just buying any woman a house like this."

"This house belongs to Trey."

"Son might own it but the mama runs it. Come on, Sam. Stop splitting hairs with the fact. Nick bought this place for you. He may not be ready for a relationship on your terms but love is a verb. The verbiage here is pretty awesome. Keep being stubborn and somebody else might snatch up that beautiful black king. Take a chance with your heart and let life flow!"

Sam kept the chain around her heart firmly in place by ignoring everything Danielle said. Easy for her to think life clear cut. She and Scott had dated off and on for years before tying the knot. Danielle had no idea what it was like to have your mind blown and body scorched by a lover like Nick, to be in the company of someone brilliant and witty and sexy and strong, and know that at any moment it could be over. That someone he felt was more beautiful or exciting could come along and take away his breath.

After the Thanksgiving holiday, when she didn't hear from him for a week and then the talk, when he made his preference for the single life abundantly clear, Sam tried to cut Nick from her heart. The longer she went without him, the deeper her feelings grew. It felt that if she ever again allowed herself a taste of him without promise, it would be like gambling with air.

Later that evening back at the condo, Sam was in the middle of a rare act—cooking. Trey had requested tacos, the one dish she'd mastered. He preferred hers to those from a drive-through. The day Trey shared this observation Sam had felt like a Michelin chef.

"Alexa, play nineties hip-hop."

Though Sam hadn't been alive when these songs were released, Sam's father Marcus was a die-hard nineties hip-hop head. It was the soundtrack of her life through high school and beyond, along with today's popular pop, neo-soul and a little R&B. While bobbing her head to the beat, Sam poured oil into a stainless-steel skillet. She crumbled up a couple pounds of ground beef, added it to the oil, then began chopping onions and peppers to add to the mix. She'd just reached for a jar of diced garlic when the doorbell rang. No one ever came to her house uninvited. Who in the heck could it be?

She quickly grabbed a towel and wiped her hands as she walked to the door. *Nick? What's he doing here? And what's he brought with him?* She opened the door and verbalized those thoughts directly.

"There is an explanation. Can I come in?"

"Sure. You probably texted me but I was in the kitchen and didn't have my phone with me."

"No, I didn't, but I couldn't help it. I got so excited about what I brought over that I headed out of the door without thinking to call."

"What could be that impor—"

"Daddy!" Trey bounded out of his bedroom and into the arm that Nick had free. He placed down the large box he carried and scooped up his son. "What'd you bring me?"

"Who said what I have is for you?"

"It's mine, Daddy!" Trey said, laughing. "You never bring Mommy anything."

"Trey, Nick brings you goodies because you're his son."

"So? You're my mom!"

Sam locked eyes with Nick. "Kids."

"Gotta love them." Nick pulled the bag open. "Actually, son, this is for your mom."

"Really?" Nick had thought to bring a gift for her? Sam's heart fluttered.

"Well…in a way."

Nick reached inside the large bag and pulled out an equally sizable box.

"What is it, Dad?"

Nick's eyes warmed as he looked at Trey's cherubic upturned face, his expression one of wonder and awe.

"Something pretty amazing."

All eyes were on the box as Nick pulled a cutter from his slacks pocket and cut the box top. He tossed protective bubble wrap to the floor, then lifted out a silver-colored head and torso with a childlike face.

Sam squinted her eyes. "Is that an r-o-b-o-t?"

Trey gasped. "It's a robot!"

Her eyes widened. Had his spelling capabilities grown that much?

"R. O. B. O. T!"

Yes, they had.

"The Academy is one of the best preschools in the nation," Nick said. "I thought you knew."

He pulled the bottom portion of the machine out of the box and now connected several wires before attaching the two parts together.

"Is it a robot, Dad?"

"Yes, but more specifically this…" He pulled a remote from the box and tapped a button. Lights began to flicker. The eyes of the robot lit up a bright blue.

"It's Ven." He tapped another button. "Ven, say hello to Trey."

There was a short pause before the robot turned to where Trey stood wide-eyed. "Hello, Trey."

The voice was not the electronic, robotic monotone Sam expected, but that of a boy who sounded about Trey's age.

If possible, Trey would have jumped out of his skin. "Mom! He said my name! He talks! He said my name!" He took a step to approach him, then stopped, a bit unsure.

"It's okay, Trey. Ven is very friendly. In fact, in Danish, *ven* means friend."

"Can I touch him?"

"Sure, come on over." Trey walked up to the machine that stood slightly higher than the taller-than-average four-year-old. "Hold out your hand and say hey." Nick sniffed the air. "Is something burning?"

"Oh, shoot! The meat." Sam ran from the room.

Nick hollered after her. "Did I interrupt dinner?"

Trey tugged Nick's hand. "Dad, we were talking to Ven!"

"Hang on, son." Nick walked into the kitchen in time to see Sam scraping the contents of a skillet into the sink.

"What's that?"

"Before the doorbell, it was ground beef. Now it's burnt garbage." Sam flicked the garbage disposal switch. "Dang it! The one dinner Trey likes that I know how to fix and I mess it up."

"What were you making?"

"Tacos."

"It's my fault. I'm sorry."

"Daddy!"

Sam looked over the bar counter at Trey's impatient face. "It's okay. You'd better finish assembling Trey's gift."

Nick pulled out his phone and sent a quick text. "Okay," he said, walking back to where Trey stood next to the robot with remote in hand.

He nodded toward the robot but spoke to Trey. "Talk to him."

"What do I say?"

"What do you normally say when you meet someone new?"

"Nice to meet you?"

"Okay. Try that."

Trey looked at Ven. "Nice to meet you."

The robotic arm began to move. Trey gasped, then giggled with delight as the arm slowly raised until the rubberized steel hand was perpendicular to his waist. The mouth moved rhythmically. "Nice to meet you."

"Wow!" Trey threw his arms around Nick's legs. "Thank you, Daddy!"

Sam looked at Nick, as impressed as her son. "Where on earth did you get this?"

"Denmark. It's the next frontier of Breedlove Bionics."

"When did the company get into bionics?"

"They didn't. Noah and I did." He shared how similar technology had helped Noah through a health crisis. The twins had been so impressed that they started their own bionics company and hired personnel to design cutting-edge products.

"Last year, when the world changed and America found millions of children home from school and largely isolated, the group began toying with the idea of robots to replace the schoolmates they could no longer interact with physically. Video games are great, but nothing beats one-on-one interaction."

"I'd say. It's almost human."

"The wonders of AI."

"Daddy, can Ven and I go play?"

"No, honey. We need to run out and get you something to eat. Or I can have something—" The doorbell rang. Sam looked at Nick. "Delivered."

He began walking toward the door. "Mind if I get that?"

Sam simply crossed her arms. Nick opened the door, had a brief conversation with whoever was on the other side of it and returned with a large bag of something smelling delicious.

"What's that, Daddy?"

"Tacos." He winked at Sam. "Your favorite."

"Yippee! Mama, can Daddy stay for dinner?"

Two pairs of identical eyes fixed on Sam. There was only one right answer, yet it took several seconds to push it through her lips.

"Sure."

Trey grabbed Nick's hand and began pulling him toward the dining table. "Let's eat." He reached his seat and turned. "Ven!"

"Coming!" The robot rolled across the hardwood floor. It stopped beside Trey.

"Sit down!"

The robot did, except there was no chair. It toppled over. Everyone laughed.

"It's a prototype," Nick offered. "Needs more work."

"If you pull out the food, I'll grab dishes and pour drinks."

"You got it."

Sam entered the kitchen feelings all sorts of ways. The scene was too comfortable, too homey, too much of what she wanted but knew could never be. She gritted her teeth, ready to pull and lock emotional bars around her heart. Then she heard Danielle.

Take a chance with your heart and let life flow.

Might as well, Sam decided. Life was heaven whenever he was around and close to hell without him. Right then she determined to stop living in the future and enjoy what happened now. An image of what could happen flashed into her mind and caused her walls to constrict. Nick had brought Trey a playmate. She was in love. Maybe it was time to let Nick be her boy toy again.

Twenty-Four

Something shifted after the night filled with tacos, laughter and Ven. Nick and Sam settled into a comfortable co-parenting flow, centered on their shared love and adoration for Trey. They began spending more time together, the three of them, at least once a week. The two who'd started out as lovers now began getting to know each other and becoming friends. Sam invited Nick to check out the ongoing new home renovation. Nick invited Sam out for horseback riding. Sam invited him to the condo for tacos she'd cooked. That night, Nick helped her stack the dishwasher before settling on the couch to watch an animated feature. Trey fell asleep before the movie ended. Nick and Sam watched it until the end. Afterward it felt totally natural to carry Trey into his room and tuck him into bed and when he turned, having Sam leaned casually against the wall watching them was the perfect portrait.

He'd almost kissed her that night.

That was a month ago and since then, his desire to do so had only deepened, along with his feelings for her. Watching Sam with Trey made his heart sing. She was an incredible mom. She was an intelligent, business-savvy, beautiful woman. She was the best interior designer in the game. And she wanted him. He could feel it, could see it in her eyes. There was only one thing in the way of their reconnecting on a deeper, more intimate level. Her terms.

Tonight, Sam had invited him to what she'd termed a "small gathering" in her new home. She and Trey had moved in the week before. He'd been in the Seychelles finalizing the island purchase and couldn't wait to get home. Tonight, he'd have two things to celebrate with Sam. His new island. Her new home. The invitation had listed dress as business casual. It had been an unusually cold winter. As Nick walked into his dressing room, he was definitely feeling the fresh newness of spring. He walked past rows of signature black and stopped at a group of clothing recently sent over by A-list fashion designer Ace Montgomery, items tailored for him from his spring collection. His hands caressed the expensive fabric as he checked out each piece, bypassing a baby blue suit of finely spun wool and a deep gold number that gave a nod to the seventies leisure suit. He paused at a pair of ivory-colored slightly baggy trousers, a sophisticated mix of sporty elegance with a fitted waist, flared pant leg and 18-karat-gold threads running throughout. Since it was still a bit cool in the evenings, a light gold turtleneck was the perfect complement to the slacks. Nick finished the look with his new favorite timepiece—appropriately called the Billionaire—and his signature three-carat diamond stud. A splash of cologne, a cigar to enjoy later and he was out the door. On the way over, he ruminated on his decision for a housewarming present. To think what he'd chosen was a good idea may prove to have been presumptive. Time would tell.

Pulling up curbside, Nick couldn't help but feel proud of Sam's handiwork. He'd purchased the house but she'd made it a home. The landscaping was impeccable, lush and commanding without being showy. Carefully placed outdoor lighting highlighted the slate siding, the redbrick walkway and the front door's stained glass. He tried the knob. The door opened. Softly playing neo-soul greeted him amid a din of cheery-sounding voices. He glimpsed himself as he passed a mirror in the foyer and noted how the five-foot floral arrangement anchored the hall just as he thought it would.

He reached the living room and stopped to look around. The first person he recognized was Sam's cousin Danielle, who spotted him at the same time, waved and walked over.

"Hey, Nick!" They exchanged a light hug. "Well, don't you look like a breath of spring!"

"Thanks, Danielle."

"Call me Danni. The other is only used if I'm in trouble or in court."

Nick chuckled. "Got it."

As they briefly exchanged chitchat his eyes scanned the room. He wasn't surprised to see faces he didn't recognize. Noah was there with Adam and Ryan, along with Larry and his girlfriend. Their eyes met, followed by a head nod as Larry held up a drink in greeting. His perusal continued beyond the L-shaped living room into the dining room, where Sam, looking like the queen that she was, sat chatting animatedly with a handsome older man.

"That's her father," Danielle offered, having followed his eyes.

"Really? He came down from LA, huh. Nice."

"Sam was very excited to show this place off." Danielle leaned in. "She may never tell you but she has never treasured anything more than she does this home. She always corrects me when I say her house—" she used air quotes "—by telling me that you bought it for Trey. That may be true legally. But a part of me says you bought it for the both of them. Am I right?"

Nick missed the last of what Danielle was saying and didn't hear her question at all. In the middle of it, Sam had looked up and seen him. Her eyes widened slightly. She said something to her father, who looked over, before rising to come toward him. She looked like an ebony goddess, draped in an ivory jumpsuit that made Nick jealous because it hugged her body the way his arms longed to do. The simple elegance of the one-piece, one-shoulder design was complemented by gold jewelry. As she grew closer, he noticed thin strands of gold beading wrapped around an errant loc. No adjective was strong or accurate enough to describe the perfection before him. His body reacted on its own. Arms reached out and pulled her into a light yet firm embrace.

"You look incredible," Nick murmured huskily into Sam's ear before releasing her. "I see you got the ivory dress code memo."

Sam smiled. Nick's penis pulsated. If his hormones continued raging, this was going to be a long night.

Sam appreciated Nick's hug and teasing comment. It gave her time to catch her breath, gather her composure and recover from seeing the man she had fallen head over heels in love with walk into the room and outshine everyone present.

She couldn't deny it now if she tried. Not after seeing

this six-foot-two-inch bundle of *GQ*-sexy stroll confidently into the room. She. Was. In. Love. With a capital *L*.

"You look good, too. I can't believe you're not wearing black!"

"It's springtime, according to the calendar at least.
Thought I'd switch it up a little bit. It seems that great
minds think alike."

"Indeed."

Danielle loudly cleared her throat. "Um, clearly I've
been dismissed."

"My apologies, Danni," Nick began, a hand to his
chest.

"Save it. I'm just teasing." Danielle reached into her
purse. "You guys belong on a magazine cover. Let me
take your picture. By the fireplace." She adjusted her
screen. "All right, here we go."

All eyes turned and conversation stilled as Nick and
Sam struck a pose.

"Give me a couple more."

They offered another angle, then Nick surprised Sam
by twirling her around and dipping her down.

Danielle squealed. "Perfect!"

The room broke out in applause. Sam was completely
embarrassed. But damn, that man smelled good.

Nick looked around. "The place looks incredible, babe.
Perfect for entertaining."

"It's exactly what I wanted. There's not one thing I
would change. Come with me. There're a few people I
want you to meet, starting with my dad. And while he's
probably not as…curious…as your mother, there may be
more than one question from him that you won't want to,
nor are obligated to answer."

"Thanks for the warning."

"Ha! Anytime."

Sam was surprised at how nervous she was for her dad to meet Nick, and how much she wanted him to be impressed by the man walking confidently beside her.

"Dad, I'd like you to meet my former business partner and Trey's dad, Nick. Nick, this is my dad, Marcus Price."

"A pleasure to meet you, sir."

Sam watched her father measuring Nick up. "Likewise."

"Considering we just met I might be speaking prematurely," Nick said. "But would you by any chance like a good cigar?"

"Why? Do you have one?"

Nick nodded. "Have you heard of the Cubano Rare?"

Marcus looked from Nick to his daughter and back. "You have one of those?"

Sam couldn't guarantee it but was pretty sure she heard reverence in her dad's voice.

"In my car. It'll blow your mind."

Marcus slapped Nick on the back and gleamed at Sam. "I like this guy already."

Sam's smile reflected how happy and relieved she was that Nick and her dad seemed like they'd get along. Because the truth of the matter was not only was she in love with her child's father, but she really liked him, too. The next time the opportunity presented itself, she intended to let him know how much.

Twenty-Five

A month after Sam's housewarming, she was on a CANN private plane headed to the Bahamas. Nick was beside her, but the trip wasn't about work. It was about their burgeoning ongoing attraction. And what they were going to do about it.

During the flight over they kept the conversation light, mostly about Trey, now truly a Breedlove, having had Nick's name added to the birth certificate and his last name officially changed. They talked about the home on a small island not far from Nassau that because of legal and other logistics had only recently been completed, and even flirted a bit. The plane's landing was smooth and once outside, they were welcomed with hugs from the balmy Bahamian wind. After a short helicopter ride from the capitol of Nassau to CANN Isle-Bahamas—the home that would be their private paradise for the next several days—the couple were minutes from their final destination. With everything about Sam having driven him wild for the past few hours, Nick couldn't get there soon enough. He and Sam hadn't yet moved out of the friendship zone back into that of lovers, but he hoped this trip would change that.

They reached the home that in luxury and originality rivaled the New York villa that was Sam's first assignment. They were met by the house staff, conferred with the chef, and went to change for an agreed-upon swim before dinner. Nick went to one of two matching master suites. He donned swim trunks, grabbed a towel and slipped into a pair of sandals. Stepping into a living room shared between the two suites, he encountered a sight that stopped him in his tracks. Sam's juicy booty, a work of perfection that was just right for squeezing, swayed rhythmically from side to side as she walked toward a patio on the other side of the room. She wore a gold-colored wrap over a bikini bottom almost powerless to fully encase her lusciousness. Its luster made her ebony skin appear all the more radiant, wrapped in a way that highlighted curves deadlier than those found in Tail of the Dragon, one of the most scenic roads in Tennessee. He'd gripped the handlebars of a rented Harley while navigating its 318 curves in eleven miles, but it didn't compare to the ride he experienced whenever he journeyed to paradise with Sam in his arms.

Sam turned, her brow arching when she discovered Nick in the room, watching her. "You coming?"

Nick's long strides quickly ate up the distance between them. "I'll come later," he whispered once beside her.

"One-track mind."

He grabbed her hand and squeezed it. "The best kind."

The two accepted refreshing adult drinks from Colin, their thoughtful chef, then made their way to a stretch of soft, white sand, miles away from eyes that might be attempted to pry. After a brief splash in the water, they settled into a sturdy hammock erected under a tree by the shore.

"Hold my drink, please?" Sam handed her drink to Nick and then shifted her body to remove the wrap and settle into a comfortable position beside him. "There, that's better."

"If we're to keep this relationship platonic, I don't know about that."

He handed Sam back her drink.

"To us and a lifetime of adventures with our son."

"Eighteen years, anyway." Sam lifted her glass to clink it against the one Nick held.

"What, after Trey graduates from high school you're running away?"

"One never knows what the future holds."

Nick took a long sip of his beverage and pondered Sam's comment. He had plans for this vacation, felt fairly sure of how they'd go. But Sam was right. In life, nothing was guaranteed.

"How's your drink?"

"Delicious. I can't believe that here where they have the best rum in the world, you chose to drink beer."

Nick shrugged. "Obviously Colin got the memo. He knows what I like." He placed his arms more securely around Sam's shoulders. "When I find something I like, I usually stick with it."

"Hmm."

Sam said nothing more but the way she moved her butt so that it brushed his manhood made Nick believe his double entendre had been received.

"I like your stick."

"Now who's bringing it up?" He lifted his head to look her in the eye.

"Must be the rum."

"Hmm." His hands began a lazy journey up and down Sam's thigh. Goose bumps sprang up almost immediately, as did his python. He kissed her temple, shoulder, cheek. "I'm glad we did this."

"Me, too. So much has happened."

"I know."

They slipped into a companionable silence. Nick placed his foot in the sand to push the hammock into a gentle rocking.

"Did you ever think we'd get here?"

"I didn't even know there was a here here," he replied. "If someone had told me a year ago that I had a son and was about to be…"

"About to be what?"

"…in a serious relationship, I would have thought them way off. I thought life was perfect. Business going great. All the girls I wanted. I didn't know my life was empty until you came back into it. And brought Trey."

"Life is crazy."

"Right."

"Want to know something?"

"Hmm."

"I almost didn't go to that party."

"What party?"

"The costume party where we met. I'm not big on those types of functions."

"Then who do I owe the million dollars to for talking you into coming? Danni?"

"It was Danni, but I'd say you owe her at least two million."

"Naw, probably more like five or ten."

Sam shifted, turned up her face. "Kiss me."

He did. Leisurely. Lovingly. Sam gave as good as she got, even outlined his mouth with her tongue when they finished the sultry exchange.

"Damn."

"Uh-huh," Sam murmured, again grazing his dick with her behind in the way that he loved.

"Okay, baby, after that and on second thought, I'll just give your cousin a blank check."

They finished their drinks and swam in the ocean. The sun began to set, splashing vibrant colors along the sand and cooling the air. They went inside.

"The next time over, we'll have to bring Trey."

"He'd love that."

"Know what I'd love?"

"Another beer?"

"Another kiss." Nick pulled Sam to the couch and plundered her mouth. She had other plans, shimmied out from beneath him and turned her body so that her mouth faced his crotch. Without fanfare or permission she slid her tongue down the length of his penis, while softly fondling the family jewels. Nick had always appreciated a take-charge woman, especially one whose treasure hovered just beneath his nose. He placed a hand on each cheek, brought her heat to his mouth and slid his tongue between the fleshy folds.

Yum.

They took their time. Sam lavished Nick's dick from base to tip, using her fingers and tongue to make his slack member steel. Nick nibbled her pearl, sampled her star, feasted on her dewy kitty until she fairly meowed. Until the dew became a fountain of ecstasy, and she screamed his name. Nick could have easily joined her in going over the edge.

But this dance wasn't over. It was just getting started. He led them into the bedroom.

He removed their clothes. They lay down, flesh against flesh from head to toe. He eased his hand between her thighs, slid his fingers into her sweet spot and began to play. They kissed, the essence of love on their tongues— swirling, dancing, flicking across the cavernous warmth until he reached such depth of passion Nick thought he might drown.

"Who does this belong to?" His breath was hot, branding, as he whispered into her ear.

"Me."

"After all that good loving?" Nick said. "Wrong answer."

Sam chuckled, her hand lazily running over six-pack abs. "Oh, really?"

Nick slid off the bed. "Get on your knees."

Sam traced a finger along his jaw. "What if I don't want to?"

Nick smiled. "Oh, you'll want to."

She chuckled and rose to her knees as instructed.

"Turn around."

She complied, her round, plump booty in the air and fully exposed. Just right and ripe for...plucking.

With a hand on each hip he eased her body to the edge of the mattress. The king-size four-poster was the perfect height for the takeover he had in mind. He watched Sam wiggle her backside. Impatient. Anticipating. But Nick wasn't in a hurry. They had all night.

Nick reached over for the glass of water on the nightstand. He took a drink, held a cube in his mouth, then quietly dropped to his knees. Instead of the warm, hard shaft she was expecting, a cold sword of delectation slid into her womanly folds.

A harsh intake of breath followed. Goose bumps appeared. She pulled her body away. But not far enough. With Nick's hands still securely on her hips, he held her body in place and continued his relentless assault. Sam swirled her hips against his tongue. He bathed every inch of intimate areas, kissed and massaged her smooth, dark skin. After she'd cried out for the second time he stood, placed his dick at her core, then slowly, oh…so…slowly, eased himself inside her. His manhood pulsed with pleasure at her tightness, even after having a kid. He pulled out to the tip, then slid in again. In. Out. Thrust. Sway. He went at this pace for as long as he could, then settled into a rhythm he could have danced to all night. On the bed. Against the wall. Out on their private balcony, where the breeze was as hot as the sex. Back in the room on a chaise, he covered her and entered her completely.

"Whose is this?" His voice was harsh, labored, as his body rumbled. He scorched her insides with passion, pressed himself deeply into her core. Over and over he loved her. Their bodies shone with the evidence of the hearty endeavor.

"Who. Does. This. Belong to?" A thrust punctuated each word that was growled.

He felt her body grip him, heard the familiar sounds that began at the base of her throat, felt her grinding faster against him.

"Ah! Oh my God!" Sam screamed with pleasure.

Nick quickened the pace, joined her in cascading over the edge. Spent, satiated, they crawled into bed.

Sam kissed him lightly, snuggling her backside against him. "You," she whispered, and fell asleep.

The deep sleep lasted just a few hours. Awakened by the hazy Bahamian sun, Nick stretched amid a yawn. He rolled over slowly so as not to awaken the sleeping beauty. Perched on an elbow, he took in her serene expression. It shouldn't make someone this happy watching somebody else sleep. A few minutes is all he lasted until he kissed her. Softly, just at the edge of her eye.

Her lids fluttered before her eyes opened fully. The look in her deep brown orbs was mesmerizing as her lips slowly morphed into a smile.

"Good morning, beautiful."

"Good morning. I can't believe you're awake already."

He nodded toward the open balcony door. "The sun."

Sam perched on her elbow and looked over her shoulder. "This view is to die for, truly paradise."

She threw her arm over Nick's body, resting her hand on his shoulder. "I think I kinda love you."

Nick kissed the top of her head. "Really?"

Sam fixed him with a look. "And?"

"You aiiight."

She reached behind her for a pillow to smack him. "Just all right?"

"Okay. Better than all right."

Sam turned her body to face him directly, adopting her sexiest tone. "How much better?"

Nick licked his lips. "Damn. A lot more. So much so that…wait a minute. I can show you better than I can tell you."

He bounded out of bed.

"Nick, where are you going?"

"Be right back!" There was the sound of rumbling before Nick spoke again. "Okay, now close your eyes."

"Why?"

"Must you always engage that beautiful brain? Just do it, woman!"

"Okay."

Nick peeked around the corner before walking back over to the bed. "Okay, hold out your hands."

"Why? Okay, never mind." Sam lifted her hands. The sheet floated away from her body. Her nipples pebbled against the early-morning breeze. Nick almost forgot what he was about to do. Change both of their lives. After which, there would be plenty of time for lovemaking.

Still, he kissed the exposed nipples before covering her up.

"You're making it hard to keep my eyes closed."

"Yeah, you're making me hard, too. You've made me a lot of things. An executive with rental properties sold out worldwide. A father to the most adorable boy on the planet. A man who's ready to stop playing around and make a real commitment."

Sam's eyes flew open.

"What did I tell you?"

"I can't keep them closed when you're talking like this! What are you saying?"

Nick reached for her hand, began stroking her finger. "I'm saying that I love you, and that I'm in love with you."

He brought the hand from behind his back and slipped a ring on her finger.

Sam was shocked speechless, her eyes tearing up as she gazed into his.

"I'm saying, Samantha Price, that I can't imagine spending my life without you and Trey, and maybe a few brothers and sisters for him to play with."

"Nick…"

"I'm asking if you'll do me the honor of becoming my wife. And that the only acceptable answer is yes."

Sam's eyes sparkled. She remembered. It's the same thing he'd said when she got offered the job.

"Are you sure that's the only acceptable answer?"

"Unless or until I hear it, we're not leaving this island."

"Well, in that case…yes, Nick Breedlove. I'd love nothing better than to become your wife."

"Good answer."

Without another word he reached over, slid the sheet away from her body and began covering it with soft, wet kisses. There were no more secrets, big or little. Tonight, there was only love…

* * * * *

#2809 TEXAS TOUGH
Texas Cattleman's Club: Heir Apparent • by Janice Maynard
World-traveling documentary filmmaker Abby Carmichael is only in Royal
for a short project, definitely not to fall for hometown rancher Carter Crane.
But opposites attract and the sparks between them ignite! Can they look
past their differences for something more than temporary?

#2810 ONE WEEK TO CLAIM IT ALL
Sambrano Studios • by Adriana Herrera
The illegitimate daughter of a telenovela mogul, Esmeralda Sambrano
is shocked to learn *she's* the successor to his empire, much to the
chagrin of her father's protégé, Rodrigo Almanzar. Tension soon turns to
passion, but will a common enemy ruin everything?

#2811 FAKE ENGAGEMENT, NASHVILLE STYLE
Dynasties: Beaumont Bay • by Jules Bennett
Tired of being Nashville's most eligible bachelor, Luke Sutherland
needs a fake date to the wedding of the year, and his ex lover,
Cassandra Taylor, needs a favor. But as they masquerade as a couple,
one hot kiss makes things all too real...

#2812 A NINE-MONTH TEMPTATION
Brooklyn Nights • by Joanne Rock
Sable Cordero's dream job as a celebrity stylist is upended after she
spends one sexy night with fashion CEO Roman Zayn. When he learns
Sable is pregnant, he promises to take care of his child, nothing more.
But neither anticipated the attraction still between them...

#2813 WHAT HAPPENS IN MIAMI...
Miami Famous • by Nadine Gonzalez
Actor Alessandro Cardenas isn't just attending Miami's hottest art event
for the parties. He's looking to find who forged his grandfather's famous
paintings. When he meets gallerist Angeline Louis, he can't resist at
least one night...but will that lead to betrayal?

#2814 CORNER OFFICE SECRETS
Men of Maddox Hill • by Shannon McKenna
Chief finance officer Vann Acosta is not one to mix business with
pleasure—until he meets stunning cybersecurity expert Sophie Valente.
Their chemistry is undeniable, but when she uncovers the truth, will
company secrets change everything?

YOU CAN FIND MORE INFORMATION ON UPCOMING HARLEQUIN TITLES,
FREE EXCERPTS AND MORE AT HARLEQUIN.COM.

The illegitimate daughter of a telenovela mogul, Esmeralda Sambrano-Peña is shocked to learn she's the successor to his empire, much to the chagrin of her father's protégé, Rodrigo Almanzar. Tension soon turns to passion, but will a common enemy ruin everything?

Read on for a sneak peek at
One Week to Claim It All
by Adriana Herrera.

"I want to kiss you, Esmeralda."

She shook her head at the statement, even as a frustrated little whine escaped her lips. Her arms were already circling around his neck. "If we're going to do this, just do it, Rodrigo."

Without hesitation he crushed his mouth into hers and the world fell away. This man could be harbor in any storm, always had been. His tongue stole into her mouth, and it was like not a single day had passed since they'd last done this.

She pressed herself to him as he peppered her neck with fluttering kisses. Somewhere in the back of her mind she knew this was the height of stupidity, that they were both being reckless. That if anyone found out about this, she would probably sink her chances of getting approved by the board. But it was so hard to think when he was whispering intoxicatingly delicious things in Spanish. *Preciosa, amada... Mia.*

It was madness for him to call her his, and what was worse, she reveled in it. She wanted it so desperately that her skin prickled, her body tightening and loosening in places under his skilled touch.

"I can't get enough of you. I never was able to." He sounded bewildered. Like he couldn't quite figure out how it was that he'd gotten there.

Welcome to the club.

Esmeralda knew they should stop. They were supposed to head to the party soon and she'd for sure have to refresh her makeup now that she'd decided to throw all her boundaries out the window. But instead of stopping, she threw her head back and let him make his way down her neck, his teeth grazing her skin as he tightened one hand on her butt and the other pulled down the strap of her dress.

"Can I kiss you here?" he asked as his breath feathered over her breasts.

"Yes." She was on an express bus to Bad Decision Central and she could not be bothered to stop.

Don't miss what happens next in...
One Week to Claim It All
by Adriana Herrera,
the first book in her new Sambrano Studios series!

Available soon wherever
Harlequin Desire books and ebooks are sold.

Harlequin.com

Get 4 FREE REWARDS!

We'll send you 2 FREE Books plus 2 FREE Mystery Gifts.

Harlequin Desire books transport you to the world of the American elite with juicy plot twists, delicious sensuality and intriguing scandal.

FREE Value Over **$20**

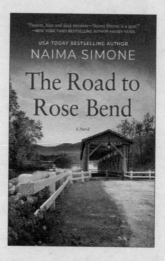